The
DISCOVERY
of
FLIGHT

We gratefully acknowledge the support of the Canada Council for the Arts and the Ontario Arts Council for our publishing program. We also acknowledge the financial support of the Government of Canada through the Canada Book Fund.

Cover design: Val Fullard
Illustrations in text by Susan Glickman

The Discovery of Flight is a work of fiction. All the characters portrayed in this book are fictitious and any resemblance to persons living or dead is purely coincidental.

Library and Archives Canada Cataloguing in Publication

Glickman, Susan, 1953-, author
         The discovery of flight / Susan Glickman.

(Inanna young feminist series)
Issued in print and electronic formats.
ISBN 978-1-77133-513-3 (softcover).-- ISBN 978-1-77133-514-0 (epub).--
ISBN 978-1-77133-515-7 (Kindle).-- ISBN 978-1-77133-516-4 (pdf)

         I. Title. II. Series: Inanna young feminist series

PS8563.L49D57 2018   C813'.54   C2018-901535-7
                                                      C2018-901536-5

Printed and bound in Canada

Inanna Publications and Education Inc.
210 Founders College, York University
4700 Keele Street, Toronto, Ontario, Canada M3J 1P3
Telephone: (416) 736-5356 Fax: (416) 736-5765
Email: inanna.publications@inanna.ca Website: www.inanna.ca

The
DISCOVERY
of
FLIGHT

a novel

Susan Glickman

INANNA

Young Feminist Series

Tell me a story, Pew.
What kind of story, child?
A story with a happy ending.
There's no such thing in all the world.
As a happy ending?
As an ending.

—Jeanette Winterson, *Lighthousekeeping*

You already know me, Sophie, so I guess you want to know about the rest of the Adler family. There are three others: my mother, my father, and my big sister, Elizabeth, who we all call Libby. Dad looks after Mum, Mum looks after Libby, and Libby just looks. Literally. Because all she can control properly are her eyes.

Libby's paralyzed; has been from birth. But you'd be amazed how much a person can communicate using nothing but her eyes if she's as smart as my sister Libby.

Our parents say that even when she was a baby they could always tell what she was thinking, because she would look at them so intently. Once she started going to school, Libby learned to communicate by blinking whenever the teacher pointed to pictures like a glass of water (meaning "I'm thirsty"), a book (meaning "I want a story"), or a clock (meaning "What time is it?"), or whatever. So Mum and Dad made their own symbol sheets at home with pictures, like of all her different sweaters so she could choose which one she felt like wearing, or a bowl of soup, or the bathtub, or our dog, Baxter.

When she was older, Libby learned to write by blinking when you pointed to the correct letters, so she could send thank you notes for birthday presents and letters to her pen pal in

Japan. She did math the same way. But this method required another person to help her, so sometimes she got frustrated. Anyone would — imagine having to go through twenty-six letters each time you wanted to spell something! I often get frustrated with how long it takes me to get my *own* thoughts out, even though I talk pretty quickly (too quickly, according to my Grandma Ruth, who can never understand anything I say to her on the telephone).

Conversations with Libby in the old days were S L O W, but things improved when her school got what they call "assistive technology": these amazing devices that help you control a computer by staring at the screen. We finally got one at home last year. I like using it; it's fun in a trippy, space-age kind of way. I wouldn't be surprised if in the future we control a lot of machines that way, or at least the lights and the TV and stuff like that. On and off at a glance. Pretty cool. So now Libby can write stories and poems on her own. Currently she's obsessed with a writing project she's working on that she refuses to show us. And she can also go on Facebook and watch videos on YouTube like any other teenager.

Of course, my sister isn't really like other teenagers because she's got cerebral palsy. According to Wikipedia, "*Cerebral* refers to the cerebrum, which is the affected area of the brain (although the disorder may involve connections between the cortex and other parts of the brain such as the cerebellum), and *palsy* refers to disorder of movement." In other words, she has problems in her brain that affect her ability to move. Nobody knows what caused those problems or how to fix them. All we know is that they began either before, or during, or shortly after birth. Which means that the major cause of cerebral palsy is being born. That's the major cause of *all* of humanity's problems, as far as I can tell.

A less polite term for Libby's condition is that she's spastic. Everyone knows what a "spaz" is, right? The girl with glasses who can't shoot hoops gets called a spaz. The boy with asthma who can't play hockey gets called a spaz. But genuinely spastic people would never find themselves on the basketball court or at the hockey rink in the first place. Genuinely spastic people can't control their movements at all; they flail all over the place and waste a lot of energy trying to put on socks or lift spoons to their mouths. Libby can't do those basic things — even swallowing Jell-O is an Olympic event for her.

Also, people like my sister can't speak clearly enough for other people to understand them, no matter how hard they try. Libby tries, she tries all the time, but she can only get out a few sounds. Like "Ba." For Libby, "Ba" is a magical word. It can mean *book,* or *ball,* or *bird,* or *boat.* "Ba Ba," is pretty obvious, right? Especially since she says it every day when the Wheel-Trans van comes to take her to school. But "ba ba" also means *pasta,* and *baby,* and *sheep,* and *bubble,* and *button,* and *butterfly.*

It's pretty cool to see how many words my sister can make with that one simple sound. My best friend Victoria Lee says that's how the Chinese language works: one sound can mean a lot of different things depending upon how you say it. (Vicky speaks Chinese at home with her parents and goes to Mandarin classes every Saturday. She is also such an authority on everything that even if she didn't speak the language herself, I would believe what she said about it.) So maybe life would be easier for Libby in China.

I doubt it could be harder. Libby's almost died a few times already and she's only sixteen. One of my earliest memories is going to see her at the hospital when she had a lung infection from aspirating food, which means inhaling it instead of swallowing it down into your stomach. This is one of the worst things that can happen to people who don't have good control of their muscles. I was four years old when my father tried to explain to me that my big sister might die. That was pretty hard to understand, even though by then I had lost my grandpa as well as a couple of Siamese fighting fish, so I knew that "dying" meant that people disappeared and you never saw them again.

Kids don't have much control over anything but still, someone going away *forever* doesn't make sense when you're little because everything else stays in its place: trees, houses, furniture. When flowers die in the winter they come back the next spring. But dead people don't come back. Not in the spring. Not ever.

September 23rd

The first time Libby almost died my mother was with her in the hospital room but Daddy and I had to stay outside, watching through a big window. Back then, I thought that part of the hospital was called the "**I See You,**" because people could stare at you even when you were too sick to look back. Now I know that "ICU" stands for the "**Intensive Care Unit**" but I still think my old version was more accurate, because Libby just lay there, hardly making a lump in the bed, with wires and tubes coming out of her. At one point she had an epileptic fit (it was her first one so it totally freaked us out; we are used to them now) and my mother opened the door and started screaming and my father and I were asked to go to the waiting room until further notice.

Somehow Libby made it through that night, and all the other nights since. She was in hospital last year for an operation on her hips that kept her in a cast for months. That was a terrible time; tears ran down her face whenever the painkillers wore off too early. But she still smiled when I came into the room and tried to join our family conversations with the few little murmurs she could make and watched everything that was going on around her with her usual interest.

My sister may not be very big but she is extremely spunky.

My friends complain when we play *Settlers of Catan* that I'm too competitive. I think I've learned to be that way from Libby. She never gives up, no matter how hard things are for her.

But although she never gives up, Libby isn't very strong. She's a stick figure strapped into a wheelchair, with these huge golden eyes that follow you everywhere. She also has very beautiful hair, rich chestnut shot through with the same gold as her eyes. I'm dark and kind of grumpy like my father but Libby looks like my mother, who is radiantly pretty. Mum doesn't fit the "dumb blonde" stereotype (I doubt anyone does). She was top of her class in economics at university and thought she might do something in government finance, but these days she works from home as a bookkeeper, because it makes her time more flexible when my sister gets sick, which happens far too often.

I wouldn't want to be one — math isn't exactly my strong suit — but "bookkeeper" is my one of my favourite words. It's the only word in the English language with three double letters in a row: double "o", double "k", and double "e". Besides which, "bookkeeper" is a very *solid* word, which is appropriate, given what it is that bookkeepers do — they pore over numbers, adding and subtracting all day long, to make sure everything comes out perfectly balanced in the end. Although if you ask me, it would be an even *better* word if we used it to describe what a librarian does!

I myself am heavily into books. Which is a good thing, because there isn't a whole lot of stimulating conversation around here, what with Libby staring at her computer, and my mother being alternatively hyper or depressed, and my father basically never home. Or when he is, he's doing physical therapy with Libby or helping Mum get her ready for the school bus, or reading his paper and blocking the rest of us out so that he can regain his strength for another day of dealing with cranky people at the municipal planning office.

So I read. It keeps me sane, and shows me how people live in other places or other times or even on alien planets. It also reminds me that there are plenty of people out there with problems, some as bad as ours.

Some even worse.

Since we are on the subject of books, I suppose I should tell you about what I like to read. I love books about kids with secret powers, or those who travel to imaginary worlds, or to different times, or all three at once. My best friend Victoria Lee and I read every book like that we can get our hands on and discuss them at great length. Some people have book clubs. I have Vicky.

Libby likes fantasy books too; I usually read to her before bed when she is feeling comfortable enough to concentrate. She has a hospital bed with a crank, so we can get the head up to a good height for reading and then snuggle close together. We've gone through the entire *Narnia* series, all of *The Dark Is Rising* by Susan Cooper, and *The Earthsea Cycle* by Ursula Le Guin. I'm going to read her *The Golden Compass* next; it's so magical, and it has a girl as the hero.

My mother claims so many authors write about boys because boys need more encouragement to read and can't identify with female heroines, whereas girls will read anything and don't have trouble imagining themselves as boys. I don't know if she's right, not having any close friends who are boys to discuss this with. Maybe if I get a boyfriend one day (ha ha) he'll tell me what he reads, and why.

Anyhow, I may or may not continue reading Libby the next two books after *The Golden Compass* when that one's done. I personally don't like the sequels as much (and Vicky agrees with me) but it's up to Libby. I usually leave it up to her whether she wants me to read more books in the same series once we've finished the first one, except I didn't for the Harry Potter books because there are so many of them and they are so long. Long books are awesome when you don't want the story to end but a pain when you have to read them out loud and it's late, and your throat is getting sore.

And obviously, she can read any book she wants herself on her computer; it's just that reading them together is so much fun. Or at least it is for me, so I assume that it is for her. Anyway, Libby hasn't asked me to stop yet, and we've been doing this since I was only six years old.

Another fun thing is keeping a journal. You would probably expect me to have done this before now, but I haven't. My Auntie Diane once gave me a fuzzy pink diary with a heart-shaped silver key, but it was impossible to take the thing seriously and I've always been a serious person when it comes to reading and writing. So I might never have been forced to confront my freaky thought-processes by putting them onto paper if Mr. Davis, my Hebrew teacher, hadn't made keeping a journal a requirement for his course. His theory was that if we all wrote down the issues that concerned us, it would "help to make our year together a meaningful exploration of our shared culture rather than a rote preparation for a ritual forced upon us by our families."

This isn't easy, given how much stuff we have to study that upsets me. For example, I'm a vegetarian because I like animals better than I like most people, but we're forced to read about which ones to eat, and/or the right way to sacrifice them to

God, who, as everyone knows, doesn't even have a BODY and therefore can't get hungry, so why they would want to devour so many innocent creatures is a complete mystery. A divine being should be able to live on stardust and psychic energy, am I right?

Still, Mr. Davis claims that animal sacrifice was superior behaviour, given that other tribes back in the day offered up humans to their gods. It's amazing how many *foolish, dull, obtuse, dense, boneheaded, blockish, doltish, nitwitted, dopey, brainless* ideas people accept without questioning (I was looking up adjectives for "stupid" to find some that aren't insulting to disabled people. Luckily there are lots of other choices, which is not surprising, given how extremely large the category of stupid people with stupid ideas is. Quite a bit larger than the category of disabled people, as it turns out). *Cloddish, half-baked, dim, lumpen, unthinking, fatuous, gormless, knuckleheaded* ideas that make me seriously grumpy. For example: the idea that everything happens to us for a reason. Try explaining that to my sister Libby! Or that we deserve whatever we get. Ditto. Or that God loves us and "only wants what is best for us."

Yeah, right. Thanks, God, for all those *wonderful* things you keep giving us like:

firefloodfamineearthquakewargenocide
heatdeathoftheuniversemathtesttomorrow.

September 26th

I'm sure I failed that math test. Sadly, it won't be the first time, and I doubt it will be the last. But by comparison to the atrocities reported in the newspaper every single day, my struggle with Grade 7 math is not a significant tragedy.

I know. This journal proves that I Have A Bad Attitude To School (not that my math teacher needs proof). But luckily, although it is compulsory, it will not be graded. According to the rubric he made us bring home to our parents, Mr. Davis "wants us to recognize the issues of most importance to us" so that we can somehow integrate them with the Torah portions we get for our Bar or Bat Mitzvahs.

I'm not convinced his plan will work. Mark Levy got stuck with a portion about the dimensions and building materials used to construct Solomon's Temple and all he's interested in in real life is dirt bikes. My portion is a little more interesting but a lot more painful: I get to talk about why God punished Miriam with leprosy for criticizing her little brother Moses.

There is quite a lot of pain and suffering in the Good Book, I have to admit. I suppose life has always been a struggle and was even harder in the days before antibiotics and cappuccinos and air conditioning. But still, I hate reading about death and destruction; I skipped many pages of *The Lord of the Rings,* for example. And I'm too squeamish to watch people get hurt in the movies even though I know that what looks like blood is just corn syrup with red food-colouring in it.

My mother is the same way, so maybe wimpiness is built into my DNA. Or maybe she's a bad role model (we were studying the difference between nature and nurture in social studies last week and that was one of the most interesting classes *ever*). My dad hates watching movies with the two of us because he has to sit in the middle so we can burrow into him from both sides whenever any scary stuff comes on.

Libby is much less squeamish than Mum and I are. Could it be because she has experienced a lot more real pain herself, so the fake stuff isn't as scary? I should ask her about it sometime; that would be an interesting conversation. The problem with talking to my sister is that she always sounds so much *smarter* than me, not only because she's older, but because what she says comes out typed with actual grammar and spelling and I babble away with "ums" and "likes" and "you knows." Which just made me realize something: writing in this journal makes ME sound smarter than I really am!

Good thing, eh?

Maybe in the future nobody will talk anymore; we'll send messages on our smart phones even when we're sitting next to each other. Some of my friends at school are like that already, I swear.

THE DISCOVERY OF FLIGHT
a novel by Elizabeth Adler

Dedicated to my sister Sophie
who has always been and will always be my best friend
on the occasion of her thirteenth birthday.

CHAPTER ONE

Aya the hawk wakes when the first rays of the sun warm the treetops. Stretching her neck, she blinks her beautiful golden eyes and cocks her head to listen. The dawn chorus has begun, and a song of praise rises through the canopy.

This is how every day begins for Aya: heat, light, and music welcome her back to her community. She likes to rest quietly for several minutes on her perch, letting the outlines of the world fill in. Remaining motionless helps her to see and feel things clearly. Those who rush around, always busy, always anxious, miss so many variations of colour and smell and sound. The sky already blue at the horizon; leaves stroking each other like green feathers; the chatter of insects under bark; the rustling of small mammals in the grass far below about to assume their struggle to survive.

Life is not much of a struggle for Aya, having no predators but humans and the occasional berserk owl. But she respects the lives of every creature, even those she enjoys eating, and is fond of imagining their daily routines: a garter snake unfurling from an impossibly small crack between boulders to bask in the warmth of the sun; a mother mouse gently washing her babies' faces with a tongue like a little pink caterpillar; fox kits scrambling out of their den, fur glowing red against the ferny undergrowth, their black-tipped ears twitching, the vivid white of their necks as they wrestle with each other. No one who lives in the forest is strange to her. Then a new sound reaches her. An unfamiliar one. Many voices, confused, crying, frightened. Curious, she unlocks her talons from the branch they have clung to all night, preens her feathers and then shakes her wings. Her body thrills to know it will soon be in motion, freer and faster than anyone else.

The noises down below first increase and then stop altogether as smaller mammals and birds take shelter at the sight of her, but the hawk's interest is elsewhere. Aya takes flight towards the distant houses of men: houses that are made of wood but strangely dense and leafless, square and flat.

What is the point of using wood — beautiful living wood — to imitate dead rocks? And why do humans insist on living together long years after their young have grown up? It seems that they are trapped in those houses, enclosures that stink of sweat and cooking food. Who would want to live like that, instead of under the stars in the fresh night air?

But today, a different smell drifts up to her. Smoke! Smoke always signals danger to the creatures of the forest so her heart beats faster, in time to her powerful wings, as she seeks its source. Grey clouds billow up at the edge of the ploughed furrows where she sometimes finds nibbling rabbits and fat field mice. And in the fields she can see many people huddled together, sobbing, while their wooden houses burn to the ground.

THE DISCOVERY OF FLIGHT
by Elizabeth Adler

CHAPTER TWO

Aya lands on a maple tree at the edge of the field to observe the homeless ones. Their grief is as penetrating as a cold wind and she fluffs out her feathers to resist it. As usual, she prefers to watch humans from a distance, grateful for the occasional meal of farm animals stolen from their settlements and enjoyed at their expense, but ready to flee if they decide to pursue her.

Humans are unlike any other creatures she knows and not just because of how they live: burrowing as though they are small and helpless, quarreling and jabbering like infants even after they are fully grown. Although they walk on two legs the way she does, they are unable to fly. Instead they run on the earth like bears or wolves, though more clumsily. And like those fierce beasts, they are her competitors at hunting, although they sometimes kill other creatures for sport — a practice that offends her deepest instincts.

Death is not meant to be a game. However much her own speed and agility thrill her when she is hunting — and to be honest, riding the sky is the greatest joy imaginable and she pities those who cannot fly — it is wrong to toy with the lives of others. Even a grasshopper has a soul, a little green soul, curious and sharp as a blade of grass.

When she was still nothing but a ball of white down nestled under her mother's warm body and her father came back with mouthfuls of beetles and worms, no matter how wide she opened her beak she was never allowed to swallow until she gave thanks. Because of her parents' insistence on respect for others, Aya has always considered humanity a thoughtless species. But now, watching the sad group clustered in the field, she feels sympathy for them. Their entire village has been reduced to a pile of ash. They must feel as she would if someone set fire to the forest — an image her mind shrinks from in horror.

And as she visualizes that scorching wall of flame rising to the heavens and imagines trees crashing down and animals screeching in pain and panic, as she feels her *own* feathers start to singe in the searing heat, she suddenly recognizes a thought reaching out to her. A single voice from the human choir, female like her, like her not yet a mother.

How she knows all this is a mystery but Aya is used to living with mystery. Hawks do not expect to understand the world, only to fly above it.

THE DISCOVERY OF FLIGHT
by Elizabeth Adler

CHAPTER THREE

The girl understands Aya's thoughts instinctively, the same way the hawk understands those of the girl. It is as though they are sisters. And it happens so swiftly. One moment there is lots of noise — a horse whinnying, a baby crying, a gust of wind rattling dry boughs, somebody slurping water thirstily — and the next, a clear channel opens into another creature's mind.

It is shocking and at the same time natural, like hearing a loved one's soft voice reading you a bedtime story. And it is oddly familiar for an experience neither of them has had before, as though this is the way communication was *meant* to be: direct and immediate, with no possibility of lying. Each knows exactly what the other is thinking, feeling, seeing, and hearing, unmediated by language or social custom.

Soul to soul.

The girl's name is Terra. She is the last child living at home, her older brothers and sisters having married and moved away to other villages, some already having their own children, her nieces and nephews (and here the hawk receives an image of big eyes, greedy mouths, flapping arms, and shrieking voices that remind her of baby birds in the nest. The young of their two species are more alike than she expected).

Terra feels a great responsibility to take care of her parents, who have always been poor and now, in old age, have nothing at all. This worry is constantly with her, a dark throbbing in the centre of her chest. It hurts her to breathe, as though she has broken a rib, whenever she wonders what will happen to them. And here they are, stumbling along with the rest of the villagers as they abandon their fields of ripening grain and vegetables, their well of sweet water, their ovens and dairies and looms. They are leaving with nothing but the clothes on their backs, carrying whatever food they've been able to scavenge, accompanied by a few frightened dogs with their tails tucked between their legs: the only animals left, since the Invaders stole all the livestock that hadn't run away. They hope to find refuge at the next village until they can return to rebuild their own homes.

When that may be, no one knows.

Terra is worried that her father will not be able to endure the journey because he is very old. Moreover, he has recently been sick and is still weak. His daughter and wife support the man's bony frame as best they can but still find themselves at the rear of the procession, just ahead of the Elders, who continue their worried discussion in low voices.

Through Terra's ears, Aya understands that the Elders are reluctant to return to their beautiful river valley because they are afraid. Despite their age and great wisdom, the Elders have never heard about people like the tattooed ones who arrived that morning before the first rays of the sun, wearing red and black masks decorated with beads and feathers. (Aya receives an image of brilliant plumage and recognizes pheasant and jay and mallard and cardinal feathers: feathers that should have remained in the wings and tails of living birds rather than covering the faces of killers.)

They had aroused the sleeping villagers, meeting them at the doorways of their houses with flaming torches and hostile cries in an unknown tongue, cutting down those who opposed them right in front of their terrified families. In the brief struggle that ensued, one Invader was killed by a villager's well-placed arrow and a couple more were wounded. Retaliation was swift; those responsible were beheaded on the spot. When the remaining villagers begged for mercy, the Invaders herded them into a field and bound them together with rope as though they were bales of hay. Four of the tallest Invaders, including one who was surely a giant, proceeded to make a pyre in the middle of the field and piled it high with the bodies of those they had slain — adding anyone who protested — while their fellow barbarians, numbering fifty or more, rode away on the villagers' horses, driving their livestock ahead of them. Finally, they had thrown flaming torches onto the thatched roofs of the villagers' houses before disappearing as mysteriously as they had come.

Why should complete strangers delight in their destruction? The Elders cannot answer this question. As keepers of the sacred books, they know that there have been many dark times before this one. History tells them that their tribe had been chased from their homeland and had a long history of wandering the earth, looking for compassion and shelter and finding little of either. They had eventually settled in this river valley, at the edge of the forest, thinking that they were so isolated that they would bother nobody and nobody would bother them. And they had lived here for many generations in peace and safety.

Until now.

But it makes no sense. Throughout history, those who had sent them into exile had always needed something: land to farm and graze their sheep on, forests for timber, quarries for stone. The wickedest had sometimes enslaved the people and had marched them away to work in foreign lands. But these new Invaders had no obvious motives, and it was this that made the Elders shake with fear. A new force had come to the land — something darker and more powerful than anything they had experienced before. Something that enjoyed destruction for its own sake.

Thinking about what I wrote last time, I realized it isn't the violence in the bible that bugs me so much. It's the frequency of genocide, i.e. *exterminating entire races of people,* as a divine punishment. I mean, seriously: Why would any god, real or imaginary, want to wipe out living beings they had created? It doesn't make any sense!

I know that God supposedly saved two of each species from the flood, as well as Noah's whole family, but still. Even if this were believable — which it is not, being mainly a good excuse for cute pairs of matching animal toys — wiping people off the face of the earth is still horrible. It reminds me of Hitler's attempt to destroy the Jews of Europe, which I never even heard about until some grisly old veteran came to school on Remembrance Day when I was nine. He talked about liberating the concentration camps after World War Two, and how millions and millions of people had been exterminated for the crime of being "different" than the majority. Not just Jews but also the Roma, and gays, and people like my sister Libby.

Everyone was upset by his speech, even the principal, who was usually about as emotional as a parking meter. I had more reason than most of the other kids to feel bad, given that my family is Jewish and my sister is disabled. But what I learned that day explained something I'd sometimes wondered about: why our family is so small. What I heard in school that day made me suspect that most of our relatives had been killed by the Nazis.

Which turned out to be true.

My mother's father was the only one in his family who was left alive after the war. His whole village was rounded up, taken to the woods, and shot, but he was saved because a kind neighbour hid him in her barn. Her name was "Zofia," meaning "wisdom"; I am named after her, which is kind of cool. When my parents finally told me this story I asked them why they'd waited so long to tell me. They said they hadn't wanted to burden me with the past, that "I had enough tragedy to deal with already in my young life."

Which made me wonder what else they were hiding. It turned out there was quite a lot. S-E-X for instance. Because Libby has never had a period, they overlooked the fact that *my* body would go through puberty. That shouldn't have surprised me, since my parents seem to forget they have another daughter, one who isn't disabled, quite often.

Yes, I feel like a bitch for complaining. But what else is a journal for if not to write down your rebellious secret thoughts?

Anyhow, to return to the forbidden topic, we're learning about the male and female reproductive systems at school this year. In separate groups, of course: the boys go with Mr. Leblanc, the gym teacher, and the girls go with Mrs. Glengarry, who normally does Special Ed. I guess you could say it is "special," learning about sex from Mrs. Glengarry, who's about a hundred years old with orangey lipsticked lips that make her teeth look yellow and a bosom that sticks straight out from her chest like a shelf. She also has tortoise-shell reading glasses hanging on a chain of sparkly beads in a sequence of two blue, two gold, and two red, over and over. The glasses sit on her bosom until she needs them, to read our tests on hygiene for instance. She reads a bit, then peers at you over her glasses, then reads a bit more, but she never says anything but "hmmm" except when she's reading from the textbook. Even so, it's hard listening to Mrs. Glengarry talk about sex because no matter how hard you try to avoid it, you find yourself imagining her having it. And that's not a nice thing for a young girl to have to imagine right before lunch on an ordinary school day.

September 30th

I think I should resist the temptation to keep on describing Sex Ed classes — even though they are hysterical and represent an aspect of my life that I think about fairly often — in case Mr. Davis is reading this.

HELLO MR. DAVIS!!!!!!!!!!!!!!!!!!!!!!!!!!

I know you said you would just *scan* our journals to make sure we were writing in them on a regular basis. But you must realize that the possibility of a teacher reading these entries will make us censor ourselves, right? I'm sure you've heard of the Heisenberg principle, which states that the fact that one is observing an experiment makes the results of the experiment unreliable.

On the other hand, if I limited myself to writing about the relevance of religion to my life this journal would be empty.

I'm a skeptical person, so it's hard for me to accept that a book put together 2,500 years ago, a book everyone admits wasn't finished for at least 500 years and that lots of different people kept adding to, is "the word of God."

If GOD wrote it, how come the first draft wasn't perfect?

Or if the problem was that people have a hard time translating heavenly speech into human language — which seems not only logical but obvious — then what makes anyone sure that the version we have is totally accurate?

(Ms. Sophie Adler's book of profound religious thought)

I have to admit that there are some good stories in there in between all the lists of THINGS WE MUST NOT SAY OR DO OR EAT and PEOPLE WITH IMPOSSIBLE NAMES AND ALL THEIR BORING RELATIVES WHO LIVED A RIDICULOUSLY LONG TIME. Like the one about baby Moses being rescued by Pharaoh's daughter and then saving the Israelite slaves even though he was raised as Egyptian royalty and could have become Pharaoh himself one day. I respect Moses because he stayed humble; he kept asking other people for help even though God made him the chief prophet in charge of a Very Large Number Of Quarreling People Lost In The Wilderness For Forty Years (which sounds not unlike the time our extended family went on holiday together...).

I also like Joseph, because he could interpret dreams. I myself have had a number of weird dreams that I wish someone could interpret as prophesies like "There will be a famine in the land, so stock up on Kraft Dinner" rather than as evidence that I need therapy. Also, Joseph tricked his nasty brothers, who totally deserved it, but then forgave them anyway, and that's another thing I wish I were better at: forgiving people. Forgiveness has never been my strong suit.

Moses and Joseph are decent, and I don't have too much trouble believing that they *were* real people once upon a time, but frankly, their stories remind me more of myths and legends than of history. Don't get me wrong. I am a huge fan of myths and legends, especially those about King Arthur, who I will probably write about in here one of these days. But even Mr. Davis admits that after the events in the bible happened they got exaggerated by later generations, so that it's hard to tell what's true and what's made-up anymore.

This is understandable, since no two people tell the same story the same way. In fact, the *same* person never tells a story the same way twice! I know that I don't. Like with my most famous story, the one about the time I fell out of the big maple tree in our backyard and landed on a flimsy plastic lawn chair so that I broke it instead of any of my own bones. I like to watch people's faces when I tell it and, depending on their reactions, I'll make it scarier (the tree gets much taller) or funnier (birds and/or squirrels are usually involved in this version).

Because it's all about getting the audience involved, right?

So now that I have your undivided attention, Mr. Davis, here's a joke I heard at recess yesterday:

A cat and a mouse died on the same day and went up to Heaven. After they cruised through the pearly gates, the mouse ran into God, who patted his little grey head and greeted him personally.

"Welcome, Little Mouse!" said God. "How do you like the Afterlife so far?"

The mouse replied, "It's seems very nice. The clouds are so fluffy and I like that soft music playing in the background. But you know what I've always wanted? Roller skates! I've been a good little mouse all my life, so now that I'm here, can I please have a pair of roller skates?'

God said, "Of course! This is heaven, so you can have whatever you want." And God gave the mouse a pair of roller skates.

The next day God saw the cat and said, "Welcome, Clever Cat! How do you like the Afterlife so far?"

The cat replied, "Oh, I'm having a wonderful time, thanks for asking. I had no idea you provided meals on wheels up here!"

October 3rd

After I told the cat and mouse joke, I realized that I left out a very important member of my family: Baxter. We like to think of him as "our" dog because my mother and father and I all walk him and play with him and pet him and feed him, but really, he's Libby's dog. Baxter is a Golden Retriever and, like my sister, he has beautiful eyes and beautiful hair. Baxter's a service dog; he had to go through many hours of special training and he takes his job very seriously. So even though I wish Baxter could sleep with me sometimes because he's so cuddly (although occasionally smelly), I understand why he has to stay with Libby to watch over her.

Baxter can predict when Libby's about to have a seizure. We're not exactly sure why, but it's probably because of his sense of smell. Dogs' noses can detect odours we can't, even in tiny quantities. That's why the police use them to sniff out drugs or weapons smuggled in people's suitcases at the airport, or send them into fallen-down buildings after earthquakes to see if there are any survivors under the rubble. The theory is that if a dog knows you *personally*, he knows what you smell like when you are healthy and can detect chemical changes in your body from diseases like cancer or diabetes or — in Libby's case — whatever it is that happens before she has a seizure. Something electrical in the brain, maybe, like a short circuit. (There can definitely be a smell when electrical things go wrong; I remember when our old toaster burned out. Maybe it's something like that.)

To be honest, I wouldn't want a sense of smell as powerful as Baxter's. I get way too much information from my nose as it is, especially taking the subway to school in the morning shoved up against some guy's sweaty armpit, or using the girls' bathroom after the janitor has been mopping everything down with that Pepto-Bismol-pink stinky disinfectant, or at the mall when my friends insist on visiting one of those stores selling expensive soap that smells like a tea-party full of old ladies.

My ears are overly sensitive too, and there's absolutely no way of turning *them* off. You can hold your nose while your father fills up the car with gas, or when the hockey team troops into school after a game and you get a whiff of what's festering in their giant equipment bags. You can close your eyes if you want to stop seeing the gross parts of a movie or video game when random heads get blown off or someone's guts stream out like bloody spaghetti or, speaking of spaghetti, the way some of the boys in my class chew with their mouths open when they're eating lunch.

But there's no way of shutting my ears, so I'm stuck hearing things I'd prefer not to hear, such as my parents arguing at night in the kitchen when they think they're being discreet. Which is a joke, because they barely lower their voices and keep smashing pots and pans or whatever. My father's the worst; it sounds like he's working at the Auto Wreckers' Yard compressing cars when he's only making chocolate pudding. Even when I put the pillow over my head (which I can't do for long because I'm afraid I'll suffocate), I can still hear them. They're usually arguing about Libby or about money, or about whether there will be enough money available to take care of Libby after they're gone. All of which is guaranteed to make me even more of an insomniac than I already am.

Something else I hate hearing: rude people the street, or in a restaurant or store on the rare occasions we manage to manoeuver her wheelchair in there, whispering about my sister behind her back. Maybe I should be grateful people aren't whispering about *me*, but somehow the fact that they're talking about my sister makes me feel bad for both of us.

Anyway, that's enough whining for now.

October 5th

Today I want to talk about Baxter some more and also draw a picture of him because as well as being a writer, I hope to be an artist some day. The best would be if I could write books and illustrate them myself.

Baxter

We got him the first time Libby almost died, as a present for her. When you think about it, it's weird that two of the beings I spend most of my time on earth with don't talk at all when I am such a chatterbox. I keep trying to use telepathy to figure out what Libby's thinking, because I'm convinced that if I were smarter or more sensitive or more tuned into my astral body or whatever, we could have in-depth conversations using nothing but brain waves. My sister also believes this, so we've experimented a zillion times with both of us concentrating really hard, but so far it hasn't worked very well. Baxter is way better than us at telepathy, especially when he wants a treat. All he has to do is stare at you and you know exactly what he's thinking.

Dad says that being able to enjoy silence is the main attraction with dogs. He used to have a Bernese Mountain Dog named Heidi. Mum was afraid of Heidi when she met her, not being a dog-person in those days. Her own mother, my Grandma Ruth — who is fussy about manners and thinks girls should wear dresses — didn't let her have any pets because she insisted that animals were dirty and didn't belong in the house. (Well, maybe they are, a little, but it's worth it.)

Anyway, Heidi was so gentle it was impossible not to love her, and smart enough not to overwhelm my mother until she was ready to be friends. She just sat a few feet away and thumped her tail every time Mum looked at her and raised her eyebrows every time somebody said her name. It was the eyebrows that Mum fell in love with; she says that Heidi had the most expressive eyebrows of anyone she's ever met, including my grandpa. And that's saying a lot, since he had the mad-professor kind of eyebrows you could practically comb.

My father used to take Heidi everywhere with him, even on canoe trips where she would climb very carefully into the boat without tipping it and then enjoy the ride, growling at ducks and loons but mostly behaving herself. She had her own special life jacket and carried a pack with her own food and water dish. Mum loves all that outdoorsy stuff too, so my parents assumed they'd keep on doing it for the rest of their lives. They tripped in Algonquin, Killarney, Temagami, Georgian Bay, and Quetico Provincial Park, and were looking forward to going farther away, maybe up to the Arctic or out west to the Nahanni. But after Libby was born with all her health problems they were afraid of being stuck somewhere way out in the bush without a hospital, in case anything bad happened. So now I'm the only one in the family who gets to go canoe-tripping, every summer at camp.

Still, we are able to take Libby into the woods in a special wheelchair with huge all-terrain tires that can roll over ice and snow and rocks and roots and pretty much anything. It cost a fortune but everyone chipped in to get it for her, including Uncle Martin, and it has changed our lives, especially hers, to be able to enjoy nature and not be stuck inside all the time watching other people do stuff she can't do and talk about places she hasn't been.

Uncle Martin has joined us a few times with his second wife, Samantha, who is at least twenty years younger than him as well as a few inches taller (especially when she is wearing high heels, which is most of the time, although obviously not when we go birdwatching). She is a lawyer in Uncle Martin's firm and is SUPER fashionable. If I grow up to be a tall and slender redhead with perfect skin (joke) she will be my style icon. Auntie Sam says you need to be well-groomed to get taken seriously in court, but she's equally elegant traipsing through the woods. I always seem to accumulate scratches and mosquito bites, a sunburn and sweaty hair, but she can clamber up and down trails in white jeans and sandals and emerge looking as fresh as a model.

My mother disapproves of Samantha because she broke up Uncle Martin's marriage to my Auntie Diane, who had a nervous breakdown after they split and hasn't been the same since. My dad and I both like her because she's a fun person, and well-travelled, and has great stories about all the places she's been — places I want to visit one day myself like Bali, and Machu Picchu, and the Galapagos. Besides, my father says that Auntie Diane was neurotic and dragged Martin down, and doesn't his brother deserve a little happiness? It's hard to argue against happiness.

Auntie Diane's grown-up daughters, Rebecca and Dana, used to disapprove of Samantha even more than my mother did, for obvious reasons, but they gave that up after Chase and Emily were born. The twins are extremely cute and red-headed like their mother, but they are only four years old and therefore not mature enough to come with us on nature walks. Even though we have to manoeuver Libby's wheelchair around rocks and fallen branches, we somehow manage to make less noise than they do! Also, whenever you go anywhere with them, they keep whining for snacks or asking for you to carry them.

I used to want children someday but now I'm not so sure.

October 6th

Although Libby may look like my mum, she really takes after my dad. She's as obsessed with birds as he is. If she were able-bodied, the two of them would be up at six a.m. every spring morning chortling over the rare migrating warblers they just added to their lifetime bird-lists and snapping photos with the telephoto lens Dad got for his forty-fifth birthday.

Unfortunately, like everything else that's fun to do, bird-watching is difficult for my sister. It's nearly impossible to focus the binoculars for Libby if we are trying to spot LBJs ("little brown jobs" in birdwatchers' slang) who zip by so fast that nobody except my father can identify them anyway. So we prefer to hike along rivers to look for ducks and geese, cormorants and herons. Waterfowl are generally large, and they mostly sit in one place or paddle around slowly so you can follow them. This makes it easier to hold the binos up to Libby's eyes so that she can figure out who is who. Also, ducks and geese — and of course swans, who can be aggressive, and are not the pretty ballerina birds people think they are — usually don't fly away when Baxter barks at them. They are used to people with pets, who they probably think of as waiters whose job is delivering popcorn, breadcrumbs, and stale donuts. Sometimes they don't even bother to swim over to inspect the food their admirers throw at them, they are already so full.

**A not-bad sketch of a swan pretending
to be a ballerina instead of a nasty bitch.**

Libby's favourite birds are hawks. Not only are they big, but also they hover in circles like kites on a string, or sit very still on telephone poles or the tops of dead trees as though they're guarding the country against foreign invasion, so you can watch them for a long time. Sometimes they spread their wings or do some spectacular aerial feat as though they know you are watching. Whenever Libby sees a hawk, her face starts to glow like *she's* the one flying! She whispers "Ba, ba!" and her body gets electric with excitement. She seems less frozen, somehow. It's hard to explain how transformed she is; you have to see it. A famous autistic scientist named Temple Grandin invented a hugging machine to help her cope with her disability. If only I could invent a flying machine for my sister!

Dad was super excited to find someone else in the family as enthusiastic about things with wings as he is (Mum tries to keep up with his obsession but she poops out after about twenty minutes, and Baxter and I just go along for the fresh air and exercise). He even bought Libby a giant coffee-table book with beautiful photos of birds of prey for her birthday last year. She has become an expert on hawks and did a really good paper on them for school with footnotes and a bibliography and everything. She is such a good writer!

I'm jealous of how good a writer she is.

THE DISCOVERY OF FLIGHT
by Elizabeth Adler

CHAPTER FOUR

Fear. Love. Anger.

These are the emotions Aya receives in waves from the girl Terra — emotions she understands very well. As a chick, she had been afraid whenever her mother disappeared from the nest and left her exposed. She had been terrified the first time she tried to fly, letting go of the edge of that high nest and launching her body into the sky — a space full of invisible currents, some warm and some cold. A space in which clouds streamed and stars shone, too high for her to reach.

The sky was unknowable, unlike her cozy nest and the nice solid trees standing all around it. Trees full of sensible animals like squirrels, who didn't try to fly. Though she'd watched her parents soar away effortlessly countless times and dreamed of lifting off like them, when the great day finally came, she panicked. Would her wings work properly? Would she stay up?

It seemed impossible. Her body froze at the edge of the nest, her talons locked as they were supposed to do only in sleep. Her mother called and called to her, lovingly. Aya could smell her mother in the soft summer air that rippled over her but still, she was unable to move a muscle.

What if she could never move again?

What if she was going to be *stuck* here, a mere observer, for the rest of her life? She supposed her parents would continue to feed her, but even that would only be possible if she could open the beak that, like the rest of her body, seemed to have been transformed to stone.

How could she bear to live like this, unable to express her true nature? She imagined the future as blue sky, vast and free, and her stuck forever at the edge of it, paralyzed. A mighty hawk rendered less mobile than a timid moth or a brainless mosquito! The thought of such humiliation horrified her so much that a cry rose in her throat, passed through her petrified beak, and reached out to her mother.

I'm coming, she said. *Wait for me.* And to her joy and amazement, her wings shook themselves free of their invisible restraints and flapped instinctively. One beat, two, and she was up in the air, her mother swooping with joy ahead of her, daring her to join the chase.

She had been terrified again on her second flight — this time not when she took off but when, landing awkwardly on a large, lichen-covered boulder, she bruised her wing and was so preoccupied by the unaccustomed pain that she didn't notice a fox creeping up on her until it was almost too late. At the last minute, her father had swooped down, screeching, and scared the predator away. In those long-ago days her father was always nearby, watching her and protecting her. But she still remembered how helpless she had felt when she smelled the fox and turned her head to gaze into its eyes — eyes as yellow as her own. Some part of her had been convinced that she was going to die, and accepted it. Her life had been so short and it was already over.

Aya shivers, remembering her terror, because fear is cold. By contrast, the waves of love she felt from her father then and feels from her human sister now are warm. Fear is opaque and white like snow or turbulent water; it moves fast, faster than thought. But love is golden and soft as sunlight. Love is diffuse; it is not a harsh beam focusing on her and making her shrink inside herself, but an embrace that gives her confidence to face the world.

The love she feels flowing from Terra towards her aged parents reminds Aya of being safely tucked under her own mother's wing, held warm against that soft chest, reassured by the steady beating of her heart. The hawk closes her eyes, reliving happy memories. She misses her mother dreadfully, having only recently gone off on her own, as is every hawk's fate. Soon she will find a mate and no longer be solitary, but until then she must be brave and remember the love given to her when she was young.

It is interesting to her that this human girl still lives in the nest with her parents; even more interesting that she feels the old ones to be her responsibility. Whenever Aya anticipates the prospect of mating, she senses Terra's thoughts hurrying away from hers. The thought is distressing to the girl because she recognizes that she will have to start a new family and leave her parents behind.

She is a good daughter, so respectful, Aya thinks approvingly.

Terra receives the thought and says, *Thank you.*

And then there is that other emotion, the dangerous one. Anger. It is red, as red as the fire that had destroyed Terra's village, red as the masks of the Invaders who lit the flames. Anger is hard to contain; it tends to get out of control, greedy like fire, consuming everything in its path — including the creature who is angry. Anger is as common as love and fear among all who live, so of course Aya has experienced it. She has felt anger at greedy owls stealing her food and destroying her nest, just as the Invaders had done to Terra and her people. An even greater anger at the farmer who had killed her dear father for carrying off one of his chickens. (Aya rarely allows herself to remember this because it gives her so much pain, but it flashes into her mind inadvertently now, eliciting sympathy from Terra.)

The greatest fear is the fear of losing those one loves and the greatest anger is anger at those who cause this loss, so the three emotions are related. Does this revelation come from Aya or from Terra, or from both simultaneously? Neither of them knows because their thoughts are so interwoven. But it suddenly seems obvious — one of those laws of nature like the relationship of night and day or the seasons. Like eating when you are hungry or sleeping when you are tired. And because neither of them can distinguish where the thought originated, the telepathic link between the girl and the hawk becomes another law of nature even though, until this moment, neither of them had imagined that such a thing was possible.

October 10th

My mother isn't big on birdwatching, like I said, but she is a serious film buff. This weekend she bought Libby the DVD of an old movie called *Ladyhawke*. It's about a medieval knight and his beloved who are put under a curse by an evil bishop madly in love with the lady himself. By night Etienne de Navarre takes the form of a big black wolf and by day Lady Isabeau is transformed into a hawk, so they can never be together in their human forms.

We all loved the movie, especially Libby, although my dad was upset because number 1) the lady turns into a *red-tailed* hawk, which is a North American bird, even though the story is set in France and number 2) he's pretty sure they kept switching back and forth between at least two — and maybe even three — different hawks in the movie. So, while the rest of us were trying to lose ourselves in the magic of cinema, he kept breaking the mood by shouting "See! See! That one has a white spot on its head and the smaller one doesn't," and "That bird has a much lighter breast than the others!" and so on.

It was extremely annoying.

I myself prefer dogs to birds (although you wouldn't know it, given how bad my drawing of Baxter was). Occasionally my father will ask me to look through the binoculars and say whether I see a black eye-stripe or yellow legs or some other important feature to help him make a decision about the species he's looking at, but mostly, while he's trying to figure out whether that's a Cooper's or a Sharp-shinned Hawk, a Pine Warbler or a Goldfinch, Baxter and I race around looking for squirrels.

When it comes to being outdoors, I'd rather go to Uncle Martin's cottage than go birdwatching. It's on a quiet lake with no motorboats and there's a canoe and kayak and a sailboat and I'm allowed to take them out by myself, which is a perfect excuse to get away from the twin noise and twin fuss of my little cousins, and the 24-hour disability network that is my sister.

My parents are happy too when we go there, because besides taking Libby into the water, which is great exercise for her and a miraculous relief from sitting all the time, they get to build fires and cook s'mores and identify the constellations and do all those nerdy canoe-tripper things they love so much. They look younger wearing their old flannel shirts and hoodies, and my dad cracks me up the way he covers his nose with a thick layer of zinc oxide because he's paranoid about getting a sunburn. They've even taken Baxter out in a canoe with them a couple of times, hoping he would like it as much as their old dog Heidi did, but he just sat there looking skeptical and whining deep in his throat. I think Baxter was too upset at being separated from Libby to enjoy himself.

Libby calls him "Baba," naturally. Sometimes the rest of us do too.

THE DISCOVERY OF FLIGHT
by Elizabeth Adler

CHAPTER FIVE

Aya quickly learns to shut her mind to Terra because the girl's thoughts are so exhausting. How can humans stand that constant *chatter* in their heads? Other creatures, even silly ones like rabbits, are more at ease in the world. Rabbits can relax and let the sweet breeze ruffle their fur; they can lose themselves in the taste of clover, the splashing of water, the busy music of dragonflies and the shimmer of their transparent wings as they speed by. Rabbits, vulnerable as they are not just to Aya and her kin but to every predator in the forest, don't waste time analyzing their chances of survival. They are too busy enjoying their brief lives.

By contrast, humans — creatures with few predators but each other — don't seem to enjoy their lives much. They worry about everything. For example, whether her hair looks nice flits through Terra's mind almost as often as whether her people ought to risk returning to their old village! She also likes to imagine what might happen to her in the future: whether she'll have any offspring and, if so, how many will be male and how many female, and what she will name them.

Surely thinking about such things is a waste of time? But when Aya gently points this out to her, the girl appears surprised; she is apparently unaware that other creatures live in the present. *But surely you need to plan ahead?* she asks. *Otherwise you will be unprepared for whatever might happen to you.*

The hawk gives this question serious consideration. Does building a nest count as planning ahead? Not really, because one needs somewhere to live. Does hunting count? Again, it would appear not; hunger is an immediate drive and once a hawk has responded to it, she doesn't worry about the next meal. Similarly, when the time arrives she will find a mate; she can't say how she will recognize him but is confident that she will. After all, she had known instinctively when it was time to learn to fly and, subsequently, when it was time to leave her parents' nest. Nature *tells* you what you need to do. No amount of thinking can change your destiny.

Terra is not convinced by these sensible arguments. Terra claims that all creatures have free will and are able to change. After all, her people now build houses rather than living in caves because they learned that living in houses was safer, and warmer, and cleaner. Similarly, they planted corn instead of simply gathering nuts and berries, and raised chickens and goats instead of hunting, because they learned that if they planted corn and kept livestock, they would never run out of food.

Aya agrees that creatures can change, but not that such change comes from within rather than from Nature. She argues that figuring out how to be safe or how to eat properly simply means that one profits from experience. If an evil owl dares to steal her nest, she will be forced to build a new and better one. If there is no more game left where she is accustomed to hunt, she will seek it elsewhere. If one stream becomes choked with weeds and its water turns foul and muddy, she must drink from another. That doesn't change her nature as a hawk. A hawk will always be a hawk and a human will always be a human.

Really? Terra asks. *Then what about us? I have never heard of a hawk and a girl communicating by telepathy before. Aren't we something new?*

Aya thinks about his. How do they know that their situation is unique?

she wonders. The fact that no one has ever told them that birds and humans can share their thoughts with each other doesn't mean it has never happened before. And anyway, she reminds Terra, neither of them sought their bond — it just *happened.* They are being controlled by destiny for a purpose neither of them understands. That being the case, they must accept the situation and live with it.

And then, exhausted from such unaccustomed speculation, she shows the girl a bush laden with ripe berries close to the path her people are trudging along. *You should feed your parents,* she reminds Terra. *This discussion is going nowhere, and meanwhile they are hungry.*

Immediately, the girl starts walking in the direction Aya indicates.

"Where are you going?" her mother asks.

"To find food," Terra answers.

"What makes you think you will find it over there?"

"Wait and see," she shouts over her shoulder, running off to find the bush she sees so clearly through the hawk's eyes. When she locates it, exactly where Aya has shown her it will be, she calls the others to help her pick the bush bare.

My math teacher is a fascist. This is not something I say lightly, being a person of strong political convictions whose ancestors had a lot of trouble with bullies. But I sincerely believe that if Mr. Fraser had the power to make us all line up and salute him or, even better, march around the school in shiny black boots and uniforms with epaulettes, he would be happy.

Except he doesn't have enough imagination for that. So instead, he demands that we sit silently at our desks copying stupid equations off the board and never ask him for explanations of anything.

$X = Y$.
Why?
How can one thing be something else?
(And furthermore, who carezzzzzzzzzzzzzzzzzzzz?)

One afternoon last week, when I came home crying after another confrontation with that creep, my parents made an emergency phone-call to the guidance counselor, who agreed to see us at five o'clock the next day "to figure out a strategy" to get through the rest of the year without me having a nervous breakdown or dropping out of school.

My Grandmother Ruth had to come stay with Libby on short notice and she Wasn't Very Happy, since she was supposed to go to a Seniors' Lecture at the Art Gallery with her Gentleman Friend, Harold, but she agreed that my Education Was Important. (If you're wondering why capital letters are sprinkled everywhere like candy on a cupcake, it's because my grandmother speaks very emphatically. Maybe that's why Mum turned out so meek.)

The guidance counselor didn't see the situation as an emergency. She agreed that it was "unfortunate Mr. Fraser disparaged my efforts to understand his lessons and made me feel inadequate." On the other hand, we couldn't expect to get along with everyone we met, could we? School was meant to be preparation for life, wasn't it? After all, someday I might have bosses or colleagues who didn't appreciate me, and I would have to rise above the situation then, wouldn't I?

She kept smiling and nodding agreement with her own rhetorical questions, so there wasn't much for me to say. What I really wanted to do was punch her to see if she would bounce back as cheerfully as she expected me to do.

Nobody who works at a school will ever admit that a teacher is in the wrong. Teachers have tenure for life unless they're found looking at child porn on a classroom computer or dealing drugs on the soccer field or something else too blatantly illegal to ignore. So this was about as much of an apology as could be expected, even though Mr. Fraser had accused me of not paying attention in class or trying to do homework assignments when I DO TRY; I try every single day. My parents witness the pain and suffering involved in that heroic struggle.

The guidance counselor also said that I am a "lateral thinker," which means that I go at things sideways and around the edges, comparing unfamiliar concepts to familiar ones.

According to the guidance counselor, there are many different kinds of intelligence in the universe and mine indicates that I am a creative kind of person. Although it's nice to hear that I'm creative and so on, she should try explaining the concept to Mr. Fraser because, according to him, my intelligence isn't a different kind, it is simply non-existent. Because in Mr. Fraser's universe, of which he is the boss, and which is made of dead rocks and poison gas instead of stardust and mystery, MATH IS TRUTH. And the truth is *obvious,* so no questions must ever be asked and he should never have to explain anything to anyone. Ever.

How can he be a teacher if he never teaches???????????

This is what I didn't have the guts to ask the guidance counselor. In school I try to make myself invisible. I have a few good friends, and a couple of teachers who think I'm smart, and that's about it. My real life is at home and at camp.

October 18th

The main problem with school is that it's humiliating. You usually haven't figured out your interests yet but EVERY SINGLE TEACHER expects you to love their class and do well in it. And every EVERY SINGLE TEACHER is offended if you don't demonstrate talent in their area of specialization, as though you're being a loser just to piss them off. (Sorry for the bad language again, but what do you expect? I'm twelve years old. Deal with it.) And then they yell at you if your mind drifts off because there are other things in your life demanding attention besides the date of some stupid war or the chief exports of a country you've never visited.

I wouldn't want to change places with my sister, believe me. Still, there are times I envy the fact that people don't keep bugging her to pay attention or to "get that sulky look off her face." Libby can imagine whatever she wants without people telling her not to be silly, or immature, or rude.

And while we're on the subject of school, here's another thing that's completely unfair. Anyone who's naturally talented at math gets 100 percent all the time, but people like me who are good in English *never* do. This means that the math brains win all the scholarships and don't have to pay for university, which is another thing my parents worry about in the kitchen at night.

Or let's talk about gym, shall we? A class which is supposed to be about fun, and health, and good sportsmanship, and all that crap, but is mostly about humiliation. Because once again, if people are naturally talented they win everything and make the rest of us look like klutzes. (Or "spazzes," which, as you know, is a word I hate, and is supposed to be politically incorrect. Although people still use all the time, especially during Phys. Ed.)

And also, this is the time of life when your body is changing, right? So a few guys are already hairy gorillas with size 12 sneakers, while most of the others look like they should still have their mittens attached to their jackets with clips. Some girls come to school in a different size 0 outfit from H&M or Urban Outfitters every day and spend recess reapplying their makeup and texting their boyfriends on their iPhones, while others — like me — still have baby fat that they try to hide under sweatshirts covered with inspirational slogans and spend *their* recesses sorting through recyclable garbage to Keep Our School Green.

I am good at sports, but Jennifer Kelly — who lives next door and has been my friend since kindergarten — is the most uncoordinated person I've ever met. She wears glasses, which might explain her abysmal eye-hand co-ordination, but she is also the world's slowest runner. If she had to get out of a burning house or away from a grizzly bear, I shudder to think what would happen to that girl. In general, she's not a competitive person except at board games, like me. We are about equal when it comes to *Settlers of Catan,* but don't mess with Jennifer when she's playing chess, or *Scrabble*, or *Risk*, or basically anything that involves strategy; she will eat you alive!

Still, I'm luckier than Jennifer because while she can help me with my math homework and explain all the stuff Mr. Fraser never will about why it's possible for X to be Y, and BEDMAS, and so on, I cannot, cannot, *cannot,* teach her to catch a ball! Her body instinctively flinches away from flying objects as though they are going to attack her. Maybe her ancestors in Ireland had trouble with arrows or spears or something; some kinds of fear are inherited in the DNA, according to a nature program I watched on TV.

You think I'm kidding? No way. For example, it's been proven that babies are automatically scared of snakes. Now ask yourself: how can they tell that snakes are dangerous rather than, say, pineapples? I mean, pineapples are *weird.* They look like angry heads without any eyes (or bodies). You have to wonder whether, if nobody told you that pineapples were fruit, it would occur to you to peel and eat one, or whether you'd be more likely to expect it to attack you.

"GRRRRRRRRRRRRRRRR!"
(Don't mess with Mr. Pineapple!)

Meanwhile, most countries in the world have myths about dragons (mostly about heroes killing them, unfortunately) and art history is full of them. There are paintings of Chinese dragons, and stone carvings of dragons on medieval cathedrals, and once I saw a beautiful glass goblet in a museum with a dragon wound all around the stem of the cup as though it were a tree or something. There are dragon bracelets and dragon t-shirts and cute cartoon dragons and stuffed animal dragons, etcetera, etcetera.

I *wish* dragons were real but sadly, we're stuck with pineapples instead. So once again you have to ask yourself an important question:

Why is humanity obsessed with dragons if they never existed in real life?

Of course, people are obsessed with God and no one has ever seen God either, so I guess being invisible is not automatic proof of non-being. Physicists know that, right? They are always trying to prove the existence of subatomic particles too small for anyone to see.

But as usual, I digress. So I will return to my thesis, which is pretty cool, if I do say so myself.

Four Reasons Humanity Is Obsessed with Dragons

and everyone reads fantasy literature secretly even after they have supposedly grown up:

1) Everyone fears **snakes** because as mammals, we're prejudiced against other critters. And anyway, scales + no legs + poison = deadly, as well as creepy.

2) Everyone fears **fire** (unless they are pyromaniacs like Brian Masterson who got kicked out of school last year for setting off Roman Candles in the teachers' parking lot).

3) Everyone fears **lions** and other predators that run faster than they do, especially when they have sharp FANGS, because no one wants to be someone else's lunch.

4) Everyone fears **things falling out of the sky** (lightning, pianos, meteors, giant tree branches) and especially things that can attack them, like eagles (extremely large birds with TALONS this time instead of FANGS, but they amount to the same thing).

Add all these fears together and you have a **four-legged, sharp-taloned, scaly reptile with wings and poison fangs breathing fire...**

THE DISCOVERY OF FLIGHT
by Elizabeth Adler

CHAPTER SIX

Terra directs the group to a field covered with soft moss and grasses where they can bed down for the night. Once the humans are comfortable, Aya flies away to hunt, then goes to sleep on a nearby tree so that she will be able to detect any threat to the girl she now considers her sister. The hawk is not used to such responsibility but promises herself that as soon as she gets Terra settled in a new home, she will resume her solitary life.

This is not to be. Flying ahead, Aya sees that the village upon which the girl has set her hopes has met with the same fate as the one she left behind. Most of the buildings are burned to the ground and there is another pile of charred bodies in a field.

What will become of us? Terra asks, trying to hide her feelings from her parents by kneeling down as though to empty her shoe of stones so that her long hair covers her face.

You will find somewhere else to live soon enough, the hawk assures her, as though talking to a little chick. *Don't worry, my sister, I won't leave you. I'll find you somewhere nicer than this. Although you probably shouldn't leave before looking around for things you can use.*

What makes you think anything useful was left behind here? Terra asks, tears running down her face.

Because I can see human tools glistening in the ruins of a barn to the right and beyond the barn, a mother goat and her kid browsing grass. I also spy a nice fat pigeon pecking for grain. Why don't you go exploring while I get some lunch?

And with that the hawk flies off, leaving Terra to witness her people's disappointment when they straggle into the village and find it in ruins. She manages to persuade them not to leave before searching for things they will need on their journey. They spend a busy hour turning over burnt timbers, moving charred furniture, and emptying cupboards and closets. Even the smallest children grow excited. The activity provides a welcome distraction from their situation and, more importantly, results in an abundance of scavenged objects and quite a bit of food.

The villagers then make several pots of fish stew and even some of pea soup. It is the first time in two days that they have had enough to eat. Once their bellies are full they resume exploring, this time discovering enough bedding (soot-covered and smelling of smoke, but warmer than what they have with them) to persuade them to pass the night in the largest barn, which has an intact roof. They agree that the strongest among them should take turns as watchmen, armed with knives and farm implements. And they settle down close together, the children playful and affectionate instead of fretful, the adults with a tremulous new hope in their hearts.

Aya, belly full of pigeon, casts her thoughts briefly towards Terra and, reassured by what she feels there, tucks her head under a wing and goes to sleep.

Since my last drawing was a dragon, this is a good time to explore my secret crush on King Arthur, who encountered a few of them back in the day. I love reading about Arthur and Merlin, and Arthur and Mordred, and Arthur and Guinevere, and Gawain and Lancelot, and even their dogs and ponies and owls, despite the fact that there are far too many stories about them — some Roman (too military), some Christian (too religious), some Celtic (my favourites) — and they all contradict each other.

Why do I have a crush on a fictional character, you ask? Well, have you *seen* the boys in Grade 7? (LOL) Still, I'm counting on you to keep this confidential, Mr. Davis. I try to maintain a certain level of cool at school, so revealing how much fantasy fiction I read and that I dream of running around in the woods with a bow of yew and a quiver of arrows would *not* be good for my image!

Arthur had this huge burden laid on him when he was young, first having to pull the sword Excalibur out of the stone and then confronting his Destiny (you have to spell Destiny with a capital "D"): bringing all those feuding lords together and giving them a Noble Purpose. He had to unify England and drive out the heathen invaders (invaders are always "heathen" for some reason, even if the folks they are invading are heathen too). Of course, Arthur had the great wizard Merlin to help him the same way Harry Potter had Albus Dumbledore, but it was his own character that earned the love and loyalty of the Knights of the Round Table.

One thing you learn if you read a lot of myths and legends is that magic can only take you so far — though I would give anything to have some myself. There's a whole lot of stuff in this world that sucks, believe me, and if I could fix it with a few swipes of my willow wand, you can bet I would.

Not that I "believe" in magic, but I love reading stories set in worlds where it exists. Usually those stories are set long ago because that makes it seem more probable that there could have been dragons and wizards back then, like Goliath and the other giants we keep reading about in the bible, or "The Sons of God" i.e., angels, or even dinosaurs, who were definitely real. And who look a lot like dragons when you think about it. Dinosaurs were the ancestors of modern birds, hard as it is for most of us to believe. Except for me, of course. I specialize in believing unlikely things. For example, I believe that my sister Libby will get better, and that one day we will be able to have an actual conversation or play a friendly game of *Settlers of Catan* or walk to the park with Libby holding Baxter's leash. Or if all of that is impossible the way the doctors keep saying it is, then at least I need to believe that someday she will stop having those horrible seizures and disappearing somewhere I can't follow her.

Because I worry that one day she won't come back at all.

So, about that dinosaur-bird connection: I don't think any dinosaurs had feathers, even the flying ones. But you don't need feathers to fly — ask a bat! Bats don't have feathers, just leathery wings. With those scrunched-up mouse faces and huge eyes, they are ugly and cute at the same time, like my twin cousins, Chase and Emily, who also have huge eyes and, according to Uncle Martin, are nocturnal.

Believe it or not, there are 986 species of bats! (That we know of. There may be others we haven't found yet.) Bats are the only flying mammals; other creatures we think possess the power of flight, like "flying squirrels," are only gliding.

Another myth: bats do *not* suck your blood. A little brown bat got into Uncle Martin's cottage last summer and Auntie Sam had a complete meltdown (she's not exactly outdoorsy; her idea of a good holiday is flying to Paris and going to art galleries, then having a cup of tea at a café where fancy ladies try not to set their toy poodles on fire with their cigarettes.) Anyhow, back to the cottage incident. My mum tried to chase the bat out of the open door by waving a butterfly net at it and singing:

Little brown bat of mine
You've got to fly outside
Little brown bat of mine
You've got to fly outside

to the tune of "This little light of mine" until we all joined in. Probably it was our singing that frightened the poor thing away! It was one of the funnier times we've spent at that cottage because, on top of everything else, my mum was sporting her pink-flowered flannel nightgown with the neck held together with a safety pin because she lost a button and never got around to sewing it back on, and a pair of woolly socks of my dad's that were too big on her, and also her face was covered with pasty white moisturizer so that she looked like a zombie at a sleepover.

As I was saying, bats are mammals. This means they give birth to little bat babies, and take care of them, and feed them milk. But pterodactyls must have laid eggs like other reptiles do. So obviously they had that in common with birds, and probably other stuff like beaks or nests or whatever. I'm going to have to search for a picture of a pterodactyl on the internet before I try to draw one because I don't remember what they look like.

When my parents took Libby and me to the museum, giant bones never interested us, no matter how many times Dad detoured to the drafty hallway of Very Large Skeletons of Extinct Animals. We always wanted to visit the bat cave and the bird room where you can pull out lots of drawers to see eggs and nests. We loved the imitation forest where creatures are hiding and you have to try to find them. But Chase and Emily have a huge collection of model dinosaurs and know all kinds of obscure facts about them. For example, that the biggest dinosaur, Brachiosaurus, was the size of seventeen elephants, whereas the littlest dinosaur, Lesothosaurus, was only the size of a chicken.

Okay, here's my attempt at a pterodactyl.

"Wheeeeeee! I can fly! Evolution rocks!"

October 26th

As you have probably guessed, I am drinking hot chocolate, which is why there is a big brown splotch on this page. Sorry. But I didn't notice what I was doing because I was thinking about how much my drawing of a pterodactyl looks like a dragon. So I looked up "pterodactyls" on Wikipedia and discovered that they had four legs like dragons, not two like birds, and some of them even had long tails! Although they were furry, not scaly, which I find kind of weird and bat- not bird-like. Pterodactyls weren't that big either; most were the size of sparrow hawks (which makes me think of Ged in *The Wizard of Earthsea*) and even the biggest ones only had a wingspan of one metre. So maybe dragons are just mythical versions of flying dinosaurs the way my beautiful sensitive King Arthur is a mythical version of some bloodthirsty warrior with B.O. and rotten teeth.

But if that's the case, how would people *know* about pterodactyls? No humans lived at the same time as they did. We learned that in elementary school and Mrs. Papadopoulos reminded us again in biology last week in case we weren't listening the first time. Dinosaurs ruled the earth during the Mesozoic Era and then died off, probably as a result of a giant asteroid hitting the planet and leaving a huge dust-cloud that blocked the sun and killed off most terrestrial vegetation (some of which looked an awful lot like pineapples, if the models in the museum are accurate). First, the vegan dinosaurs died out, then the carnivorous ones at the top of the food chain. Kind of the opposite of what's happening in the modern world of genetically-modified food sprayed with cancer-causing pesticides, where all the toxins get concentrated in hamburgers and bacon and lamb chops (I'm sorry; the mere *thought* of eating a lamb makes me want to cry) so that people who eat them are poisoning themselves. Whereas those of us who refuse to eat our four-legged cousins are healthier.

Or so we hope.

Anyhow, humans didn't arrive on the scene until much later, when the climate was better and stuff was growing again, and they could be sure of getting five daily servings of prehistoric fruit and vegetables. (Unless you think the bible is literally true, which some people apparently still do, though it's hard to understand how they can ignore all the scientific evidence of evolution. But people have believed much weirder stuff than that over the course of history, for example that sacrificing a child would make crops grow, or eating your enemy's heart would give you his courage. Or that if you prayed to God, your sister would get better.)

So here's the thing that makes no sense. If people *weren't* alive at the same time as the dinosaurs, if no frightened cavemen saw a pterodactyl swoop by and tried to swat it with his club, how could caveman mummies and daddies tell scary stories about them to caveman children? How could descriptions of giant flying lizards get passed on generation after generation?

Well, maybe fear of dinosaurs is still in our DNA because it was transmitted from those tiny mammals who were biting Tyrannosaurus's ankles back in the day: mammals that are our ancestors the way Tyrannosaurus is our Thanksgiving turkey's ancestor. That would be awesome, wouldn't it, if those legends about dragons are actually prehistoric mouse-memories of pterodactyls!

I have to draw another picture now. I hope it isn't cheating to fill my journal with drawings, Mr. Davis. Tell me if it is, okay? But I thought we were supposed to represent our true self and *my* true self likes to draw stuff. Especially weird stuff like this:

**Great Great Great Great Great Great Great Great Great
Great Great Grandpa
about to suffer a miserable fate!**

Also, I know I said yesterday that I was going to write about King Arthur and ended up discussing how many species of bats there are instead, but that's typical of the way my so-called mind works. After the guidance counselor said I was a lateral thinker, I looked the phrase up on the internet and was disappointed to see that most of the entries were about how grownups should use lateral thinking to solve problems in business rather than how kids could use it to survive math class. But one of the techniques suggested reminds me of me: you're supposed to pick a random object and then connect it to whatever problem you're thinking about to find an unexpected solution.

Sadly, my randomness never solves any problems. It just gets me in trouble. For example, in history class when we were studying the French revolution and I asked the teacher what they did with people's heads after they guillotined them: did they bury them separately from the bodies or together with them?

Anyhow, I'm too distracted today to even pretend to be logical. Libby has started having terrible seizures again after a couple of relatively quiet years. The doctor put her on a newer and stronger medication, one that's only been available for a couple of years so that nobody knows whether there will be long-term side effects. The new drug seems to reduce the intensity of the seizures (though not how frequently she has them, which is almost daily now), but it also makes her extra tired. So, she's either working on that secret project on her computer she won't tell us about or she's sleeping.

I miss her.

And I'm scared.

THE DISCOVERY OF FLIGHT
by Elizabeth Adler

CHAPTER SEVEN

The villagers decide to stay where they are a little longer to figure out what to do next. Some would be happy to rebuild on this very spot. Many houses have foundations undamaged by fire, and the forest nearby is thick with hardwood to cut for new lumber. The river is full of fish and its banks contain red clay with which to make bricks and pottery. There are fields full of grass for their flocks and rich black earth ready for farming. And, best of all, this new village is on a hilltop with good views of the surrounding countryside, so they will never again be vulnerable to a surprise attack.

In addition, if they settle here, they can leave their bad memories behind. This is also why they are confident that the original occupants of this village will not return and displace them — they too must have moved on, leaving their grief behind, because it is the right thing to do. But even if they *do* come back there will be plenty of room for them, this being such a spacious settlement. And if they do come back they will be welcome, for there will be greater safety in numbers.

A second group argues that, on the contrary, the former inhabitants will surely return and be angry to find strangers living in their village. They anticipate being kicked out and finding themselves homeless again, this time with winter coming on. So they want to return to the land upon which many generations of their families have been born, and in which many generations of their families have been buried. If they are prepared to rebuild, why not rebuild their *own* village?

Besides, their crops will be ready to harvest any day now. Perhaps some sheep and goats escaped and will have wandered back, needing food and water. They can almost hear their poor animals calling to be milked, see the corn tossing its silk in the breeze, and smell the beehives overflowing with golden honey and the purple grapes ripening on the vine.

A third group wants to abandon the region entirely and flee as far as their legs will take them, because they are convinced that the Invaders will come back one day and kill them all. They believe that staying here shows not determination but passivity. They refuse to lie down and wait to be slaughtered. Only in completely new territory will they be able to raise their children without being haunted by terrible nightmares.

Because there is so much dissent, the Elders appoint representatives for each group and promise to hear all their arguments at noon the next day before arriving at a decision. Until then, they encourage people to keep looking for useful items, especially food and weapons; to bathe children and assist old folks; to mend their shoes and clothing; and above all, to pray for unity so that they will be able to build a new life together — wherever that may be.

Aya perches on a treetop, listening to all this chatter through Terra's ears. It makes her head hurt. Hawks would never disagree about this issue; their instincts being highly territorial, they would rebuild their old nests if possible and, if not, build new ones close by. Though she hasn't built a nest yet herself, Aya knows how to do it. First you have to find a nice tall tree with good sightlines in all directions. Then you pile dry sticks into a cleft between branches to create a large platform with a deep inner cup. Finally, you line the cup with bark and grass to make a soft bed for your eggs to lie in.

But then she considers the location of their previous homes, in a flat river-valley with no vantage point from which to scout the landscape. It is true that the villagers rarely bother to hunt, relying instead on domestic livestock for meat, so they don't need to see their prey from above the way that she does. But still, their low-lying situation had made them vulnerable to predators; look what had happened to them! So maybe they *shouldn't* go back home. Because everyone knows it is safer to be high up, and this new village is located higher up than the old one.

Weighing options like this is a new experience for Aya, and she isn't sure she likes it.

How can you stand thinking about every little thing like this? she asks Terra.

It's all I know, the girl replies. *It's how we humans are.*

Well, it's not how hawks are! My brain is getting as tangled as a wild grapevine. If you need my help, Sister, I will return, but for now, the sky calls.

That sounds wonderful, Terra laughs. *I will send my mind along with you for the ride.*

November 1st

I never thought this day would come. Libby doesn't want me to read to her anymore. Obviously, it's a good thing she's enjoying that secret project, so it's bitchy of me to complain. Still, apart from feeling hurt — which I admit is selfish — I don't like the way it's tiring her out. She keeps working until she's exhausted or has a seizure, then spends the rest of the day withdrawn from everyone and everything, in her own little world.

My father hasn't offered to take her birdwatching for a while either, because the weather has been cold and wet and she seems even more fragile than usual. He keeps watching that stupid *Ladyhawke* movie with her instead, even though Mum and I are sick of it. Fantasy in general is much better on the page than on the screen. Especially when it comes to old movies, because the special effects were so bad back then. Have you ever seen the original *Doctor Who* television series? The evil Daleks — who are supposed to be most terrifying villains in the universe — look like vacuum cleaners. When they chant "Exterminate!" "Exterminate!" all I can think of is that they are going to do an excellent job sucking cat hair off somebody's carpet.

Also, like a lot of old movies, *Ladyhawke* has a loud soundtrack that tells you what you are supposed to feel about what you are about to see. I hate it when movie music does that. It's the same with laugh tracks on TV. I mean, *really?* If something is scary, I promise that I will be scared. If something is funny, I will laugh. As the writer or producer of the show, your job is to deliver the drama. You don't have to coach the audience how to respond to it as well, thank you very much.

We know you think we're stupid from the ads on TV. You think that that seeing a car being driven across an exotic landscape will make us want to buy one, or watching people drinking beer will persuade us that alcohol consumption leads to popularity. My father says studies show that advertising works, but I have trouble believing it. But then again, I'm someone who refuses to wear clothing with brand names on it. If people want me to promote their products, they should be paying me to wear them and not vice versa!

Clearly, I'm a *crosspatch (curmudgeon, sourpuss, malcontent, bellyacher)*, i.e., an argumentative kind of person. Which is why when it comes to *Ladyhawke,* my favourite character is the thief, Mouse, who spends quite a bit of time quarrelling with God. I can't identify with the female protagonist because Michelle Pfeiffer is too beautiful. She is so beautiful that every guy she meets falls in love with her at first sight and is willing to fight to the death to win her, etcetera, etcetera, etcetera. She is the kind of beautiful that makes ordinary mortals want to wear a balaclava to school.

But unlike me, my sister is beautiful. And like the Lady Isabeau, she is under an evil spell. So I understand why this movie appeals to her so much. But still, ENOUGH WITH THIS PLOT ALREADY! How about a guy falling in love with someone because she is a good conversationalist, or shares his passion for lawn bowling or online role-playing games? Why must your looks always be your most important attribute? It would be amazing if someone made a movie about a totally awesome girl who was not beautiful but who men fought over anyway because she was interesting and so much fun to be with.

However, I doubt that will happen in my lifetime.

It's amazing how much my sister Libby looks like Michelle Pfeiffer! Or would, if she were older and somebody plucked her eyebrows and put makeup on her. Her nose isn't exactly the same, and her lips are a bit thinner, and she has a lot of freckles. But otherwise.

Maybe that's why Libby barely breathes when the sun rises and shines through Lady Isabeau's delicate fingers and makes a golden halo around her golden face and then the camera pans away and we hear a hawk screeching overhead and when the camera returns, TA DAH! She has been transformed into a hawk. When Libby watches that scene she is so enraptured it's like she is praying. When I watch it, all I can think is: *What happens to the lady's clothes when she becomes a bird?*

First, I tried to copy a still photo of Michelle Pfieffer from the movie to put into this journal, but then decided I'd rather draw my sister Libby. This taught me two important things. 1) I suck at drawing people, and 2) it's a lot easier to copy a photograph than to draw a living person because the photograph has already transformed a three-dimensional body into a bunch of lines and shadows on a flat surface.

In the days before photography, portrait painters didn't have that option; they had to make their models sit still for hours and hours while they worked. What happened if someone had to go to the bathroom? And if the models had to come back another day, how could they make sure they were in exactly the same position as before? How could they be sure that their hair and skin would look exactly the same as it did the last time? I get new pimples every single day. (Mum keeps swearing that no one can see them but me, but I don't believe her.)

Or imagine trying to paint a self-portrait back then. You would have to keep looking into the mirror and then away from it to copy what you saw. But when you looked back at the mirror you'd see that you'd moved, so you would have to erase what you just drew and then redo it only to find, *next* time you looked in the mirror, that you'd moved once again.

How anyone has ever finished a self-portrait is beyond me! Probably the reason Rembrandt made so many paintings of himself was that none of them was accurate.

Anyway, I shouldn't be writing in this journal tonight because I have a TON of homework to do and already wasted two hours on horrible portraits. But this is typical of me: the more work I have, the more I procrastinate. But my teachers also procrastinate: this week, they all suddenly remembered that they need us to complete at least one major project before exams so that they can fill in those pesky report cards. You'd think they could schedule things better after being in this business for so long — after all, November follows October on every single calendar. But planning ahead would mean putting students' needs first, and who ever heard of that?

Most teachers don't even *like* students, which makes me wonder why they decided to go into teaching in the first place. Probably to have two months off each summer off so they can do the things they really enjoy, whether that's something exciting like going backpacking in India (like you did, Mr.

Davis, but as I've already noted, you are cool) or something ordinary like taking cooking lessons (my French teacher does that every summer, and when she talks about making a chocolate soufflé, she's way more enthusiastic than when she talks about the *plus-que-parfait*).

That would be the main attraction of teaching for me: having summers off to do fun stuff. Because, to be honest, I don't like children that much either. I would definitely need some chocolate-soufflé-making-and-especially-eating to recover from the trauma of dealing with their crap all day long.

Not counting the continuing horror of math assignments — which even Jennifer Kelly is getting fed up with — I have to do a book report for English on *Great Expectations* (okay, that's easy), a French translation (boring), an essay for science on global warming (scary), and a history project on European exploration of the Americas. For history, I have to collaborate with a boy I don't even know named Malcolm West. He seems reasonably smart from the few things he's said in class but still, I don't like collaborative assignments. Most of the time I end up doing most of the work because my partners promise to do stuff but don't. And then I resent their getting good marks because of my efforts, or me getting bad marks because of them.

Anyway, you would think that was quite enough homework for anyone to cope with but I also have to learn how to chant my Torah portion — a great privilege, as my mother keeps reminding me, since she never got to have a Bat Mitzvah herself.

Privilege? Are you kidding? Sorry Mr. Davis, because I know this is your thing, but let's get real: NOBODY enjoys learning how to chant their Torah portion. It's so off-key and whiny that you feel like a human bagpipe. Even Baxter leaves the room when I'm practicing and he's a service dog, trained not to react to ambulance sirens!

Is "bagpipe" even correct in the singular? I stopped writing this journal to look it up on the internet and discovered that wind instruments made out of sheep's bladders originated in the ancient Middle East and are mentioned in the Torah — which doesn't surprise me in the least, because the most peculiar things tend to turn up there when you are least expecting them. Like unicorns (Numbers 23:22), and four-legged insects (Leviticus 11:20-23), and God showing Moses his "backside" (Exodus 33:18-34:9); you have to admit *everybody* in our Hebrew class laughed at that one, Mr. Davis. And p.s., I should get extra marks for looking up the exact references for this stuff.

What's even worse than having to chant Torah is the thought of performing it in front of a crowd of people who have been sitting uncomfortably for hours, waiting for you to make a mistake, before rewarding you with a fountain pen or some other token of Becoming An Adult. And then — when The Big Day is over and you think you are finally, FINALLY, FINALLY going to have some free time — you still have to write about a million thank you notes by hand.

Which must be why so many people give you fountain pens. But one pen is quite sufficient. So if anybody asks you what *I* want, please tell them to get me gift coupons for books, okay? The prospect of enlarging my library is the only thing that makes the ordeal worthwhile.

November 5th

PS: I promise I will give money to charity too, Mr. Davis, after I save some for university and pay my parents back some of what they are spending on this shindig. Because lunch after the service is going to be *soooooooooooooooooooo* expensive! I overheard my mother discussing it with Grandma Ruth, who is lobbying for "a tasteful affair" with smoked salmon instead of tuna, and mixed greens with balsamic vinaigrette instead of coleslaw, and the better-quality linens, etcetera, etcetera. When Mum reminded her that we can't afford to be "tasteful," Grandma Ruth offered to pay for the flowers and the tablecloths and "a selection of elegant pastries" herself.

As usual, my grandmother's suggestions came off sounding like criticisms and made my mother even more nervous than she already was. So after Grandma Ruth left, I told Mum that we should forget about the Bat Mitzvah, since none of us needs any extra stress. I also said that we should save our money because we will need it to take care of Libby. Maybe there will be some new kind of treatment for her in the future; you never know. And new medical treatments are usually expensive, especially if you have to travel to get them.

I'm serious about this, Mr. Davis. I couldn't stand it if we wasted our money on a party for me instead of getting help for my sister! It's bad enough that I already get to do so many things she can't like making art, and going canoe-tripping, and playing board games, and simple everyday stuff like brushing my hair or turning off the Classic Rock radio station when Mum starts singing along to it. I feel guilty all the time that Libby's older than me but hasn't experienced half of the activities I have. It wasn't so bad when I was little, but the older I get, the worse the gap between us becomes. That's why spending so much money to celebrate some archaic ritual is ridiculous; we ought to be saving up every single penny to help *her*.

But my parents won't accept this argument. They keep saying that "we all need something happy to look forward to." I keep replying that I'm not looking forward to having a Bat Mitzvah and that I'm not happy about having one. But as usual, my opinion doesn't count.

THE DISCOVERY OF FLIGHT
by Elizabeth Adler

CHAPTER EIGHT

One after another, representatives from the three factions make their case: to rebuild the village where they are; to go back home; to keep travelling until they find somewhere new. When they have finished talking, the Elders retire to a small grove of beech trees to consider the options. The sun is still high in the sky and the weather unusually warm for autumn. Not knowing what else to do while awaiting judgment, the rest of the villagers go down to the river to wash their clothes and fish for dinner.

Despite everyone's anxiety, the atmosphere is festive. Time stands still between summer and winter, between the past and the future. For once, there is absolutely nothing to do. The villagers feel oddly free, as though they are on holiday rather than in exile from everything they know.

Terra settles her parents on a fallen tree where they can sit comfortably and watch the surrounding activity, then wanders down to the riverbank where a few children are splashing around, hooting with excitement. She takes off her own shoes and wades in. The water is cold but she soon grows accustomed to it, flexing her tired feet and smiling with pleasure at the tiny minnows nibbling her toes. A frog jumps off the riverbank and a kingfisher swoops by, wings flashing blue, breast the red of a ripe apple. She stirs up the sand and the minnows swim off, carrying away the worry of the past few days. It is so beautiful here! She would be happy to stay, and it would be better for her parents not to have to travel again. The journey here has exhausted them, especially her father.

She hasn't heard Aya's voice for many hours and wonders where she's disappeared to. Perhaps the hawk needed to take a break; their communication is more disturbing for the bird than it is for Terra herself. Echoes of other people's voices are a constant chorus in Terra's head and her memories of the past are as vivid as the present. But soaring into the sky and seeing objects become small and insignificant through the bird's sharp eyes has made her realize how very different their lives are. How uncluttered everything is for the hawk.

On the other hand, Aya is so solitary. Since she'd left the family nest more than two years ago, she has been on her own. Terra can't imagine living this way; she is sure that loneliness would lead her to despair.

But Aya claims she is happy because she is free. What might such freedom be like for a human? Is it possible to live completely by yourself and for yourself? Could you *have* a self separate and distinct from your friends and relations? In Terra's world, those who try to be free from attachments and obligations are either holy or mad — cave-dwelling hermits praying in silence, or beggars sleeping outside in the cold, filthy and disease-ridden.

Besides which, humans aren't the only social creatures: lots of animals live in herds or packs — not only tame ones like cattle or dogs, but also deer and wolves. Fish swim in schools; she'd just experienced that. And all around her the trees are alive with sparrows and starlings and blackbirds, flitting from branch to branch and chatting amongst themselves. Aya may enjoy solitude but clearly most birds don't.

Meanwhile Aya is far away from Terra's ruminations; far from the villagers and their endless troubles. The day remains warm and the sky brilliantly blue, so she keeps flying until she becomes so hungry that she must find food. A down-draft brings her soundlessly lower to the earth, low enough to hear something rustling in the yellowing grass and Michaelmas daisies, and she is about to swoop down on a quail when another hawk dives out of nowhere at lightning speed and snatches it from under her beak.

How rude! she thinks. Surely he must have seen her circling there, about to make her kill?

Sorry, Miss, he thinks back at her. *I was concentrating so hard on catching this bird that I didn't even notice you. But you are welcome to share my meal.*

She lands beside him and cocks her head for a better look. Being a male he is smaller than she is, but he is quite handsome nevertheless. His wings are much darker than hers, making a nice contrast with his fluffy white chest; his tail is brick red above and orange below; his eyes are as golden as her own. Obviously, they belong to the same species and are roughly the same age.

Didn't your mother teach you any manners? she teases him.

Yes, but they've grown as rusty as my tail since I left the nest, he replies. *Come on, join me. I can see that you are hungry.*

Half a quail isn't much of a meal! she retorts.

Then you'll have to help me hunt for something else once we've finished the first course. Then he moves aside courteously to make room for Aya, and waits for her to take the first bite.

She is intrigued. It is too early for her to seek a mate; she will have to wait until the spring for that. Still, this male seems both healthy and intelligent, and he hasn't found his partner yet either.

What do they call you? he asks, as soon as they have finished eating.

Aya, she replies, after wiping her beak delicately on one wing. *And who are you?*

I'm Shay.

Well, Shay, if you want us to hunt together you will have to keep up with me. But I'm not sure you are strong enough to do that! And she flaps her great wings and speeds off as fast as she can.

He is right behind her, and if she had thought flying alone was fun, flying with a friend is even better. She inscribes giant loops on the sky, daring him to catch her, then doubles back and dives towards the ground at tremendous speed before stalling and swooping up again. But Shay is equally agile and equally competitive; wherever she goes, he appears as though by magic. The sun sinks lower in the sky and the shadows lengthen and still they fly together, crying out with excitement so that smaller birds flee in terror and rabbits hide in their holes, until finally he calls to her that he is still hungry; isn't it time they finished their meal?

We probably scared any prey away with all that screeching, she replies.

Follow me, Shay says. *I want to show you a technique I learned from my parents. They used to hunt together all the time.*

When they reach the edge of the forest, he indicates that their destination is a crooked pine tree. Then he speeds towards it, shrieking once again, and flushes a squirrel from its leafy nest high in an upper branch. The panicky animal runs down other side of the tree into the grass, where Aya easily catches it.

We make a good team, Shay declares.

Yes, we do, Aya agrees, rather amazed at what has just happened.

November 8th

I went to the drug store to buy some not-tested-on-animals shampoo and they were already playing Christmas carols. A day or two ago, the shelves were full of discounted jack-o'-lantern napkins and vampire fangs and fake blood. Obviously, smart people should buy their seasonal supplies the day after each holiday and stick them in the attic until they need them. Most packaged Hallowe'en candy wouldn't taste any different a year later anyway, it's so full of chemicals.

My dad says that when he was a kid, everyone on his street started the night's trick-or-treating at one particular house because the lady who lived there made homemade caramel apples and they ran out quickly. Another house on his street offered popcorn balls, and his mother (my Grandma Elizabeth, who I never met because she died before I was born) liked to bake cookies or fudge. Those kinds of treats are worth going door to door for, IMHO. But these days, everyone is so worried about kids getting poisoned or finding needles in apples that they won't let their neighbours make anything tasty.

What a world, what a world! to quote the Wicked Witch of the West, which is who I went as this year.

This is not as much of a weird segue as you might think because we had a Hallowe'en theme at our house this year.

We all went as characters from the *Wizard of Oz*. It was my mother's idea. When she was growing up, that movie was on TV every year during the winter holiday and her family watched it ritually, so now she makes us do the same thing.

In case you haven't already noticed, my parents are very into "togetherness." (This is one of the reasons I spend so much time at Victoria Lee's house, by the way: *her* parents leave us alone. They are too busy with their careers to play board games with a couple of twelve-year-olds.) But to be fair, my mother doesn't dress Libby and me in matching outfits anymore. This time we decided to do it all by ourselves!

Libby went as Dorothy in a blue gingham dress and white apron and red slippers, with her hair in pigtails, and Baxter walked beside her wheelchair with a sign on his back saying "Toto." My dad dressed completely in grey so that if anyone asked him who he was, he could say "The Tin Man." Unfortunately, I don't know if anyone asked him. Vicky and I left the others behind right away because they were too slow (probably because everyone on the street had to stop and pat Baxter).

Vicky was dressed as Madame Curie, her idol. She borrowed a lab coat from her mother and embroidered "Marie" on the pocket. It wasn't until it got dark outside and she started to give off an eerie greenish glow that I realized how good her costume was. She'd dribbled fluorescent paint all over her lab coat to represent the fact that Madame Curie was exposed to unprotected radioactivity and eventually died from it. She also had glow-in-the-dark gloves on her hands. Most of the people whose houses we visited got the reference, and gave Vicky extra candy for being clever. Sometimes I don't give that girl enough credit!

The reason we got separated from my father and sister so

quickly was that we couldn't wait to see the haunted house around the corner where a bunch of actors live. Those guys are super creative; they do something amazing every year with props like flying bats and smoke machines and it's a real highlight of Hallowe'en. Even the mums and dads in the neighbourhood have to go check them out; they pretend it's to see whether the special effects are too scary for little kids but really, they want to get in on the fun themselves. This year there was a guy dressed as a mummy standing on the roof moaning and another one lying in a wooden coffin in the front yard who kept popping up and scaring everyone. It was *way* cool.

Anyhow, when we left the haunted house we didn't see Dad and Libby, so we went on without them. We came back two hours later, our pillowcases bulging with seriously unhealthy treats. This is our ritual: we pour all the candy onto the living room carpet and sort it into piles and then do a comparative count of what each of us has (12 Crunchy Bars, 10 Mars Bars, 4 Coffee Crisps, 6 boxes of Smarties, and so on) so we can trade stuff. I hate jelly beans and lollypops and Vicky's allergic to peanuts; we make a perfect team in this way, as in so many others.

Still, we felt terrible when we found out what had happened to Dad and Libby. They didn't make it very far, just up one side of the street and down the other, because Libby started shivering and spacing out, and Baxter started getting alert and nervous like he does when she is about to have a seizure, so my father took them home. And she did have a seizure, a really bad one, but Dad said he was glad we kept on enjoying ourselves because, realistically, there was nothing we could have done to help anyway. Mum turned out the porch light even though it was only seven p.m. so that no more trick-or-treaters would ring the doorbell, and the two of them put Libby to bed and sat with her.

And that was that.

November 20th

The school said Libby has to stay home for a while because she's having too many seizures. She's really upset, because she loves school. Also, because she's too exhausted to eat and can't be trusted to swallow properly anymore, she had to go into the hospital for a couple of days to get a tube put into her stomach. And even though the gastric tube was supposed to take away our worry about making sure she gets enough to eat, it hasn't. Because dripping stuff into a hole in your stomach doesn't seem like eating, does it? And we feel terrible sitting down to dinner when she can't join us.

She's also back on a catheter, which is humiliating. And because she's stuck in bed most of the time now, my parents bought her a new mattress that's supposed to redistribute her body weight so she doesn't get bed sores, which are much MUCH worse than they sound, believe me. People — especially paralyzed ones like Libby — can die from them. So Mum is vigilant about turning her every two hours when she's lying down, which Libby hates. We all hate it, actually, because it means that nobody gets to sleep through the night. Even though my parents take turns moving her and they don't ask me to help, we all seem to wake up anyway.

All of which means things are majorly tense around here.

Forgive me if I don't write much today. It's too hard to be funny or eloquent. I'm even too tired to be sassy, which is usually my default mode.

THE DISCOVERY OF FLIGHT
by Elizabeth Adler

CHAPTER NINE

The Elders make their decision with exceptional speed. The nights are getting colder and the days shorter; time is not on their side, and they know it. If the villagers keep looking for another spot as good as this one — somewhere with fresh water, arable land for farming, pasture for their livestock, and a geographical position that makes it easy to defend themselves — who knows when they might find it? And once they do, they will have to build shelter for approximately a hundred people before winter comes. Can they be sure of obtaining sufficient timber or clay in another place? Will they have enough time?

The Elders do not think it likely.

Here they have both materials and foundations upon which to build. They have more extensive fields than they used to, a larger orchard, and a river filled with fish instead of a well. The only things they lack are the terrible memories that would surely haunt the old place and fill every waking hour with fear. Staying here will be a perfect compromise between trudging back to a lost past and marching off into an unknown future. Best of all, when the snows arrive in a couple of months they will not only be protected but will have stored enough food to sustain them until spring.

The villagers accept this decision with remarkably little grumbling. The beautiful weather of the past few days now seems a cruel illusion; the Elders' reminder that winter is on its way shocks them into a frenzy of activity. Carpenters scrutinize the ruins to see which houses are salvageable. Able-bodied teens and adults are recruited to gather all the reusable material and sort it by length and size and type: large timbers in one pile, small ones in another, ropes over here and stones over there, wedges and nails and dowels in another place. Three of the fastest runners are sent back to their old village with wheelbarrows to bring back whatever useful items they can find there: food, clothing, furniture, tools, or even stray animals. A group of old folks go down to the riverbank to make clay bricks as well as vessels for cooking and for carrying water, while Terra and three other young people start to build a smokehouse to cure fish. Some of the most responsible children supervise the younger ones in harvesting whatever is still ungathered in the fields.

You are very busy, my sister, Aya suddenly remarks, landing in an old oak tree on the other side of the river.

We're going to stay in this place after all, Terra replies, startled at hearing that familiar voice in her head once again.

I know you think we should return to our old nest, Aya, she continues, *but the Elders have decided that this is a better location for us. So we have to make shelters before the snow starts falling. My parents and I are going to live with our old neighbours and their two little boys. Their grandparents may have to move in with us as well.*

That nest you are building looks too small for such a large group, the hawk observes skeptically.

This is not for us to live in! Terra says, laughing out loud so that the girl working beside her looks up curiously. *This is going to be a smokehouse for fish, to preserve it for the winter.*

You need to learn to hunt, my sister. A good hunter like me can find fresh food all winter long.

Sadly, we've been farmers so long we have lost the skill.

I will teach you how to hunt, the hawk insists. *Then you can teach the others.*

Maybe later, Aya. Right now, I need to finish this building.

Is there anything else I can do to help you?

Yes, there is, Terra replies, thoughtfully. *If you can keep an eye open and let me know if you see the Invaders — or anyone else suspicious — coming this way, I would be very grateful.*

That is a good job for a hawk, Aya replies proudly. She pauses, as an image of Shay floats into her mind and with it a warm feeling that takes her by surprise. *I will ask a friend to help me,* she adds. *He's a good flyer too, with excellent vision.*

Who is he? asks Terra.

Shay, Aya says, embarrassed at how much pleasure it gives her to say his name.

December 3rd

Malcolm West has turned out to be an excellent person to work on a project with. Not only is he not a slacker, he's smart, and not only is he smart, he gets things done on time.

The reason I didn't know this before is that he only moved to this neighbourhood last summer, after his father started teaching full-time at the university. Malcolm's father teaches keyboards and the history of music, and conducts the student jazz band as well as being in a trio himself, so he's extremely busy. Which is why we have been working on our "Europeans Stealing Land And Resources From Indigenous Peoples" project *chez moi*. My folks don't like the idea of us being at his place without adult supervision.

This is funny because: a) we are totally into our work, which currently involves making a *papier maché* diorama of Christopher Columbus's ship, the Santa Maria, sinking on the coast of the island of Hispaniola, and b) Malcolm has given no indication that's he's noticed I am female. Still, I'm flattered that anyone thinks a guy as good-looking as Malcolm West might put the moves on me!

We chose Hispaniola for our project because it was the first permanent European settlement in the Americas, and the way the Spanish exterminated the native Taínos and then brought slaves from Africa to work on their plantations set the pattern for their other colonies. Also, Malcolm's mother was born in Haiti, the country that forms the western half of the island today. The other half is occupied by the Dominican Republic, which I'm sure you know, Mr. Davis. At first I thought it was weird that a single island was divided into two completely different countries but when you think about it, the continent of North America is just a giant island and it's divided into Canada, the United States, and Mexico.

Anyway, Haiti is one of the poorest countries in the world so Malcolm's grandparents left there to provide a better life for their kids, like mine did from Europe. Malcolm doesn't have many relatives here, another thing we have in common. His dad is white, so Malcolm's got beautiful skin that always looks tanned and dark eyes and jet black hair as a compromise between his parents.

Malcolm lives with his father and his older brother, Carl, who is in his senior year of high school and could theoretically supervise us if we worked on our project over at his house. But Carl is never home because he is a musical genius who plays about a hundred different instruments. He's in a lot of ensembles as well as the city's youth orchestra. Malcolm says that Carl will probably get a scholarship to Julliard or somewhere like that when he graduates, but the only way his absence will be noticed is that there will be more food in the fridge.

Malcolm is not into music as much as his brother and his father are. He says he is decent on the piano but not serious about it, even though he's already passed his Grade 10 conservatory exam. I've never heard him play, although we have a piano in our living room that mainly serves as a place to display photographs. Anyway, he says he prefers the guitar because it's "friendlier and more portable" (his words). I will get to hear him next term when his band, *Manatee Patrol,* will be performing at the school talent show.

Why is it called *Manatee Patrol,* you ask? Well, the group's drummer, Alex, visited his grandmother in Florida last Christmas and they spent the entire holiday visiting different spots along the gulf coast trying to spot manatees. He claims the critters were often mistaken for mermaids in olden days, which I find hard to believe. Take a gander at the band T-shirt.

(**Not** the little mermaid)

Alex is obsessed with manatees, and because he did a project on manatees for science last year, even I know that they are related to elephants and as smart as dolphins, able to remember complex information, and communicate with a wide range of sounds. Also more obscure facts, such as: they have three fingernails on each flipper and when they get into shallow water they walk on their nails, and mother manatees suckle their babies in their armpits.

I have to admit that manatees are charming. They are the only marine mammals that are completely vegetarian, so they spend half the day sleeping and the other half swimming slowly around, blinking their tiny eyes and looking for plants to eat. Malcolm likes them because the name "manatí" comes from the lost language of the Taínos, the original people who lived in Haiti where his mother's family comes from. In fact, that's what persuaded him to let Alex give the band that name.

On a more serious note, Malcolm's mother died two years ago of ovarian cancer. The doctors didn't catch it until it was too late because she didn't have any obvious symptoms — just a backache, which everyone assumed was from working too hard as a physiotherapist. His father could afford to spend a lot of time on the road performing because his mother made good money. But after she got sick he started teaching more so that he could be home to take care of her and the boys.

I didn't find this out until last week, when we were at my house after school working on our project. I knew Malcolm lived with his father and his brother but I assumed his parents were divorced, like the parents of at least half the kids I know. It never occurred to me that something terrible had happened to his mother. Meanwhile my mum has taken an indefinite leave from her job to look after Libby, so she kept hovering around all afternoon offering us cookies and cups of tea, and she asked him a lot of personal questions.

Also, because our project was spread out all over the dining room table, we could see Mum going back and forth between Libby's room and the kitchen, where she was making some kind of curry and vegetarian samosas (whenever Libby isn't well she gets into obsessive cooking; her way of dealing with stress. Dad and I don't mind a bit). So my sister's condition was pretty hard to ignore. Maybe knowing how sick Libby was made Malcolm feel less uncomfortable talking about his own situation than he would normally have been. It's not that Malcolm is *shy* or anything, but he's self-contained. He's okay with people not knowing who he is or what he can do; he genuinely doesn't care what anyone else thinks about him.

If only I could be more like him! I get depressed when I think I'm not being appreciated or I'm being misunderstood, both of which seem to happen way too often. I'm not sure why. Maybe I look younger than I am, so people don't take me seriously. Or maybe I feel older than my age because of everything I've been through. Or maybe just I joke around too much, so everyone thinks I'm not really as sensitive as I am.

Vicky thinks that's the real problem. She appreciates my morbid humour, but most people don't. They don't get that life can be funny AND tragic at the same time, like in those old *Road Runner* cartoons my dad loves, where an anvil falls on Wile E. Coyote's head and you're supposed to laugh even though obviously it's not funny for Wile E. Coyote.

Why I make jokes about sad things: when the anvil falls on me I may be crushed by pain, but I see the funny side too.

December 5th

For as long as I can remember I've seen myself from the outside, like a character in a movie. Day or night, asleep or awake, there's always some kind of commentary running through my head. Even when I'm dreaming there's a part of me that *knows* I'm dreaming. Like the director of a movie, I can decide whether it's a good dream or not and, if it's not, I can revise it. Or try to. If for some reason I can't change the script — usually because I've already forgotten the events that lead up to the point that is upsetting me — I wake myself up in frustration.

If only I could direct my everyday life the way I direct my dreams! Then I could rewind to when the school bus still picked Libby up in the morning and we used to take her birdwatching on the weekends and I read to her almost every night. Back then I felt bad for her because her world was so small, but since her seizures have gotten so bad, it's shrunk even more. Because of the feeding tube, we're not supposed to give her anything by mouth. Sometimes we let her suck on a popsicle, but that's about as exciting as things get for my sister these days.

I already mentioned that she's not allowed to go to school because they say it's too much responsibility when she's this sick. But the worst part is that she doesn't even *care*. Libby used to love school; she couldn't wait to go each morning.

And all her teachers adored her. They said she was brilliant, a pleasure to teach, etcetera, etcetera.

It's not just school. It's everything. Like I said, she doesn't want me to read to her anymore. When she has the energy, she works on her secret project, otherwise she sleeps. Meanwhile her doctors are running out of new drugs to try. They keep telling us there's great new research taking place, but what good does that do us? We're running out of time.

THE DISCOVERY OF FLIGHT
by Elizabeth Adler

CHAPTER TEN

Aya watches Terra's people curiously as they work from dawn to dusk putting new walls and roofs on houses, harvesting the fields and picking fruit-trees, cleaning and sharpening tools, washing and mending clothes. Other large predators spend most of their time sleeping, but humans are busy throughout the daylight hours. And not only here in their new village. Small groups have crept back to their old homes and returned with the kind of things they like: bits of metal and wood, vessels to cook their food in, farming implements, and so on.

The biggest prize had been a wagon, garlanded with flowers and filled to the brim with booty, pulled by two homesick horses who had run away in a panic when the blaze began. The horses were as happy to see people they knew as the people were to see them. A few other animals had also been found roaming the perimeter of the village: several chickens, two geese, one bewildered cow, and three matted and filthy sheep. The cow and sheep trailed behind while the chickens and geese squawked indignantly from inside the wagon.

Aya too is busier than usual. She has enlisted Shay to help her keep watch and they spend their days, together and separately, flying over wide swathes of countryside. Foliage is flaming red and gold, growing brittle, and falling from the trees. Fields have started to turn brown and often, in the early morning, they wear a skin of frost. Like the villagers, creatures everywhere can be seen building shelters and stockpiling food. Mammals are growing winter coats and putting on layers of fat; their meat has become tastier than ever, sweet and rich from all the berries and nuts they have been eating.

At night, the hawks roost in a splendid oak tree on the far side of the river. It is obvious that they are destined to become mates once spring comes since neither has any inclination to look for another partner. Shay has not been able to develop a telepathic link with Terra no matter how hard he tries; he and the girl are forced to speak to each other through Aya, who quickly realizes that this is a good way to entertain herself at her friends' expense. For example, when Terra asks Aya to ask Shay if he has seen "anything suspicious" on the slope of the western mountains, Aya mischievously translates her query to "anything delicious." Terra is puzzled when he answers that he has eaten a snake but prefers mammals to reptiles, but eventually figures out that Aya has altered her question deliberately.

I don't think you are mature enough to have a boyfriend, Aya, she says, shaking her head.

He's not my "boyfriend."

He's a boy and he's your friend. Therefore, he's your boyfriend.

You are just jealous because you haven't found a mate yet, the hawk retorts.

I am too busy to think about such things. When life returns to normal, there will be time to think about marriage.

You're already thinking about it, Terra. I know you like that fellow with curly hair and dark eyes like a raven.

Adam? Of course I like him. I've known him since we were children!

You no longer like him the way one child likes another.

Can we change the subject, please?

You introduced the subject of mates in the first place, my sister.

You really are becoming like a sister, with all this teasing! Terra laughs. *I thought it would stop after my older siblings left home. Little did I know I'd have to put up with an annoying bird instead.*

Would you prefer that I fly away? Aya asks, insulted.

No, no! I didn't mean to hurt your feelings; this is the way human sisters talk to each other. How do you talk to your siblings?

I only have one brother, the hawk replies. *He was a very greedy nestling. My mother always had to feed him first or he would make a fuss. I haven't seen him since he fledged. Until I started talking to you, my life had been lived in relative silence.*

Don't you talk to Shay?

Occasionally, but we prefer to look and listen. Why don't humans do that?

I don't know, Terra sighs. *I wish we did. Most people just talk to hear their own voices.*

Why? Few of them sing very well.

You're right about that! Terra replied, laughing.

December 12th

Malcolm and I got an "A+" on our history project. No surprise; some of the kids in our class act like they are still in elementary school, where printing stuff off the internet and then sticking it onto coloured poster-board with a glue-stick is all that teachers expect. Meanwhile, we had *three* parts to our well-researched summative:

1) The diorama, complete with *papier-maché* waves covered with tiny white beads for foam, real sand and shells on the beach, palm trees I made from scratch with green felt fronds and reddish-brown beads for coconuts, and a spiffy pirate ship from a LEGO set Malcolm had when he was a little boy.

Because ask yourself: what's the difference between Christopher Columbus and a pirate? Not much. He stole booty from people at sword-point. He spread disease wherever he went. And he was as cruel as any buccaneer, chopping the hands off Taínos who couldn't afford to pay him tribute.

2) A power-point presentation with actual *facts*. Did you know that Columbus had no clue what he was doing when he set out to find an ocean route west from Europe to Asia? He didn't know America was in the way, and he estimated the distance as six times less than it is, so if all that land hadn't been there, he and his crew couldn't have survived with the

amount of food and water ships were able to carry back in those days. But he pretended that if he called the land he arrived at "The Indies," no one would notice that he never reached his real destination.

**The Santa Maria,
the most famous pirate ship ever! Yo Ho!**

Also, a Spanish priest named Bartolomé de Las Casas wrote in his *History of the Indies* that after the Spaniards landed on Hispaniola, "from 1494 to 1508, over three million people perished from war, slavery, and the mines. Who in future generations will believe this?"

(Well, since the Nazis managed to kill eleven million civilians and prisoners of war in an even shorter time, I guess our generation has no problem believing this, do we, Mr. Davis?)

3) A *real* bibliography with actual BOOKS on it.

I'm as addicted to the internet as the next kid (I defy you to find *anything* more entertaining than a sloth. Except baby sloths having a bath or eating flowers.) Still, scrolling down to a key-word and then cutting and pasting stuff does NOT constitute "research." And Malcolm agrees with me about this — after all, his father is a professor! Also, Malcolm's a good writer, like I am. Maybe even better.

(BRILLIANT IDEA)
**I should ask Malcolm to write my Bat Mitzvah
speech for me!**

December 15th

Just kidding, Mr. Davis! I wanted to see if you were still reading this journal because if not, why should I keep writing it? There's so much other exciting stuff to do around here. Like making a colour-wheel out of my pencil crayons, and matching single socks.

Except for that **A+,** life is pretty grim right now. And no, it *doesn*'t make me feel any better to think about the winter break. Because Victoria Lee's parents are taking her to Mexico to visit Mayan ruins and eat mangos and lie on the beach, and Malcolm and his father and brother are going skiing at some fancy resort that has an awesome indoor water-park, and some of the kids in my class have cottages where they can curl up in front of a roaring fireplace and drink hot chocolate, but my family isn't going anywhere, not even up to Uncle Martin's place like we always do for Libby's birthday — which is conveniently the day before New Year's Eve, so it kind of blends together into one big celebration — because this year Libby is too sick to travel (or anyway my parents are worried about being too far from the hospital, which amounts to the same thing)?

I think that was the longest sentence I've ever written, and it was extremely enjoyable figuring out how to punctuate it. (Don't you dare tell anyone how much I like punctuation, Mr.

Davis! That's a secret between you and me, okay?)

I recognize that complaining about not going away on vacation makes me sound like a spoiled brat, since Libby is the one who is suffering. She won't even be able to enjoy her birthday party this year. But listening to teenagers whine is the risk you run if you ask us to write down what we actually feel. Because if we write down what we are really feeling and not what we *think* we ought to be feeling, you're going to have to hear a lot of "Poor Me!" instead of inspirational stuff about how to save the planet.

Okay, that's about all the self-pity I can stand for one afternoon. Back to saving the planet. Which I want to do, except I don't know how. I suck at science, or at least the math part of it, so I don't think I'll be able to stop global warming, or cure cancer, or even help people like Libby communicate by telepathy, even though that would be the most awesome job of all. But maybe I can become an investigative journalist and either uncover conspiracies and corruption or communicate scientific discoveries to non-scientific types like myself.

This journal has been useful, because I've learned that 1) sometimes I don't understand what I think or feel until I write about it, and 2) even though writing about it may not solve anything, it makes me feel less helpless. So thank you for assigning this project. Despite complaining that it takes too much time, I'm enjoying it. And it's great to have an excuse to write and draw and call it homework!

THE DISCOVERY OF FLIGHT
by Elizabeth Adler

CHAPTER ELEVEN

Terra waits until the walls of her house are chinked with moss so that no cold drafts can blow through. She waits until sturdy roof beams have been installed and a thick layer of thatch tied down securely on top of them. She waits until a solid new door swings easily on its oiled hinges. And then she asks for permission to go back to their old village to look for the sketchbook she was forced to leave behind.

At first her parents refuse to let her go, arguing that no object so flimsy could have survived the fire. But Terra reminds them that her sketchbook was wedged between the hearthstones to keep its pages flat, and therefore may have been protected from the flames.

In the end, Terra's parents agree that she can go. She has always been the most compliant of their children, rarely asking for much; certainly not for anything unreasonable. They are unable to refuse something that means so much to her. Perhaps they might be less nervous if they knew that her guardian hawk would be accompanying her, but it does not occur to Terra confide in them. How can she explain that she can communicate telepathically with a bird? Surely they will think she has gone mad and send for the Healer, an ancient crone with rotten teeth who will poke her and prod her and burn incense and chant nonsense.

Or is she reluctant to tell them about Aya because she can't bear to share this experience with anyone else? Terra's rapport with the bird is the only thing in her life, besides the lost sketchbook, that is exclusively hers. The need to make art had appeared one day when she'd poked a finger into the flour her mother spilled on the table in preparation for kneading dough. From then on, it had become unstoppable. She had scratched images in the dirt with a stick and onto the fireplace with stubs of burnt charcoal. She had designed animals with pebbles and acorns and flowers, and portraits of her family out of buttons and pins and scraps of cloth. Recognizing her talent, the village scribe showed her how to make paper by soaking grass and squeezing the fibrous pulp through a screen so that it dried in sheets. She had sewn many such pages together to make a sketchbook she could carry about with her, the book she had left behind in the rush to leave their burning village.

Her relationship with Aya hasn't replaced Terra's need to make art. On the contrary, it has increased that need, because now she is able to see the world through the brilliant eyes of a hawk: eyes ten times better than her old ones, eyes that can detect a mouse in the grass from a mile away and perceive ultraviolet light. She wants to record these wonders while she can, in case the magic stops as suddenly as it began.

Terra dreams of making two related series of illustrations — the world as seen by a hawk and the world as seen by a girl — depicting, for example, the same tree from different perspectives, the same house, the same hillside. The river from its banks, sparkling through a fringe of reeds and bulrushes, so full of life: frogs, fish, turtles, dragonflies, everything small and busy; the river from above, a blue snake moving sinuously across the still landscape. The horizon as the vanishing point when you look across a field of poppies towards a distant snow-topped mountain; the sky as another kind of field in which clouds graze like sheep before shattering into prismatic water drops when the sun strikes them.

Aya can't understand why this idea excites her friend so much. Why does Terra feel compelled to copy what she sees? Images are not real. You cannot eat a picture of food. You cannot sit in a picture of a tree. You cannot smell a picture of a flower. A picture of a bird cannot fly. It is obvious to the hawk that such pictures are less real than memories, less real even than dreams.

Terra first tries to make Aya understand art by comparing it to birdsong, but this is a touchy subject for hawks, who cannot sing. Then she compares it to nest-building, but her friend rejects that comparison as well, insisting that a good nest is merely functional, a place for eggs to hatch. A nest does not aspire to beauty.

Finally, Terra makes the analogy to flight: hawks fly in search of prey, true, but they also soar into the air purely for their own pleasure. They *enjoy* flying and challenge themselves to become better at it, more daring, faster, more graceful. Aya concedes this point, although she isn't sure that either the experience of pleasure or the pursuit of excellence makes flying a form of what Terra calls "art."

Well, maybe it's your form of art, Terra suggests, *and drawing is mine.*

If that is true, I understand why you need your sketchbook, my sister. I will accompany you on your journey to find it.

THE DISCOVERY OF FLIGHT
by Elizabeth Adler

CHAPTER TWELVE

They set off the next day. Shay stays behind, reluctantly, to watch over the villagers. He wants to come too but he has promised to stand guard, and a hawk never goes back on his word. Terra asks Aya to stay behind as well because she is convinced that a small group of travelling teenagers is less likely to be attacked than the settlement, but the hawk refuses to listen.

Tell Shay that I give in, Terra sighs. *As usual, you're the boss.*

Terra says that without me, you'd be lost, Aya says.

I doubt it, Shay replies, having finally understood the rules of the game.

He says "undoubtedly," Aya reports.

Terra shrugs, and gathers together a few things for her journey. Her mother presses extra food and blankets upon her and gives her the warmest jacket they own. Her father gives her a sharp knife to tuck into her belt, having made her practice throwing it until her arm is sore.

The Elders insist that, in case of trouble, they must always travel in pairs. For that reason, they always send four people on these scavenging expeditions. Terrra will be travelling with two boys and a girl who is slightly older than she is. The girl has made the trip before and is the leader of the expedition; she sits at the front of the wagon and urges on the horses — not that they need much direction, familiar as they are with the route back to the old village. One of the boys has also been scavenging before and is a skilled archer, so he is positioned beside the driver, bow and arrows at the ready to defend the team. The other boy, Adam, is the same one Aya teased Terra about. She dreads what the hawk will say once she recognizes who is sitting beside her in the wagon. But she can't sense the bird anywhere in the vicinity, so she feels able to have a conversation with the boy without Aya overhearing them.

"Even though I know it will be upsetting to see what the village looks like now, I'm excited to go back there," Adam observes, "Because it's an adventure."

"Me too," Terra agrees. "And best of all, this trip means we get a break from constant supervision. I miss the freedom I had in the old days to go where I wanted and do what I felt like doing."

"Freedom? I can't even remember what that was," he sighs.

"How is your living situation?"

"Not great. The people we are sharing the house with have a baby who cries all the time. I can't wait until we get our own place."

"Me too. Too much togetherness can drive you crazy."

"Well, if we didn't know the meaning of community before, we certainly know it now."

They both laugh at this observation and then sit in silence for a while, enjoying the quiet of the countryside and the occasional flash of a bird in the treetops or a rabbit hopping through the underbrush. The trees are mostly bare except for a few last yellow leaves, but the sky is bright blue and the light golden as honey. As soon as the sun goes down they will become chilled, but for now they can drowse lazily in the sun's warmth.

"How long until the first snow, I wonder?" Terra asks.

"Soon," Adam replies. "We'll have two or three cold days, and then an equal number of warm ones. Those are the best days of all, a memory of summer at the end of the autumn, but they never last."

"Nothing good ever lasts," Terra declares bitterly.

"Why do you say that?"

"Look at what happened to us!"

"But we survived, and now we're living in a better place," he says. "Life is change, Terra, and sometimes change is good. We were so lazy before; we believed that everything we needed to survive in this world had already been discovered by our ancestors. Now that we have been forced to improvise, we are inventing new tools and new kinds of building techniques. We have been freed from the weight of tradition. Even our food tastes better, somehow."

"Well, you certainly have an interesting way of seeing things, Adam. I wish I was as optimistic as you are."

"If you spend more time with me maybe it will rub off," he says, shyly putting his arm around her.

"Maybe it will," she replies, blushing, but allowing herself to relax into his embrace nonetheless.

And by the time Aya appears overhead to check on the progress of the travellers, Terra has fallen asleep with her head on Adam's shoulder, lulled by the rocking of the wagon and comforted by his presence. If hawks were able to smile, Aya would definitely be smiling.

This has been the most BORING holiday ever, so there's nothing for me to write about. Mum said I should make use of the so-called "vacation" to work on my Bat Mitzvah speech, even though I don't need it until the end of May. So while most of my friends were racing down ski-slopes or drinking exotic fruit juice out of pineapples (they don't look nearly as scary decorated with paper umbrellas), guess where I was?

At the library.

By myself.

Which is where I am right this minute.

Although it's a lot more cheerful here than at my house these days, what with Libby in some kind of trance and completely uninterested in anything going on around her — including me — and my parents not even bothering to keep their voices down when they "discuss" things anymore, and Grandma Ruth clippity-clopping in and out in her high-heeled shoes with Horrible Hairless Harold in tow, clearing his throat and looking disapproving about pretty much everything. At least when Grandma showed him some of my new drawings he said that I "showed some indication of talent." Coming from him, that's a rave review.

Grandma and Harold took me to see *The Nutcracker,* which was magical, especially at the beginning when the Christmas tree grew enormous and all the toys under it came to life. I really didn't think I was going to enjoy seeing a ballet because 1) I had to be nice to Harold, who paid for the tickets, and 2) I had to get dressed up, not that I mind dresses but pantyhose are the work of the devil, and 3) the girls at my school who dance always seem so snobby, like they think they're better than everyone else. If you ask them to do anything after school or on the weekend the answer is always, "I can't. I have dance." Besides which, any girl who wears her hair in a perfectly neat bun and considers a small container of fat-free yogurt a satisfying lunch is annoying, but a whole gang of them doing stretches in the hallway during recess are super *extra* annoying! But watching the ballet made me realize that if those girls already know that dancing is what they want to do for the rest of their lives, school is kind of irrelevant to them — or even more irrelevant than it is to the rest of us.

This is not to say that they don't need some kind of education; obviously they don't have the skills to survive on their own yet. But bunheads have to put a huge amount of effort into dancing or they will never become good enough to do it professionally. In fact, watching the ballerinas on stage doing things with their bodies nobody normal can do made me realize that if I want to be a writer, I need to start working harder on my writing.

Which is why I agreed to work on my Bat Mitzvah speech even though this was supposed to be a holiday.

Which is why I spent so much time at the library.

December 28th

Our branch of the public library is my real place of worship, Mr. Davis, even though it's full of little kids stampeding around in muddy boots and big kids checking their Facebook accounts and flirting and homeless guys seeking refuge from the cold in those big cozy chairs by the window that I would like to curl up in myself. Still, spending the whole winter break at the library would have been depressing, so I signed up for an art course at the community center.

It was great. At school, everybody thinks art is a fake class where you get to play instead of working. But art is as much work as any other class if you try hard. At my course I learned about shading, which is something I didn't understand properly before. It's not just a matter of being able to copy what's there in real life, because sometimes in real life the light is too diffuse and there aren't any good shadows to give your work "dimensionality" (love that word!). But if you understand the principles involved, you can fake it; you can *pretend* that there's a strong light source and then put the shadows in the right place. And then BAM! your drawing looks better.

It's pretty cool.

Here's an example of what I mean. I'm copying it off something the teacher handed out. It's a sphere with a light shining on it. It's not out in space like the earth being shined on by the sun; it's sitting on a solid surface, like an orange on a table.

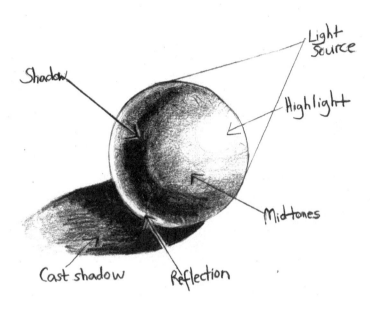

This sphere is my best one yet, even though I had to erase it and redraw it five times. We spent an entire class drawing ping-pong balls and mine were totally pathetic — they looked like rotten mushrooms (I hate mushrooms. They always taste like wet paper). But the teacher said that geometric shapes are harder to draw than ordinary objects like fruit or shoes or whatever because they don't occur very often in daily life and therefore have no context and no associations. What that means is that if you draw a red apple, people think "I'm hungry," or if you draw some running shoes they think about their favourite sport, so your drawing has more meaning to them.

I reread what I wrote about putting in fake shadows when there aren't any clear ones on the objects you are trying to draw, and how the fake shadows make the drawing look more real, and realized that's exactly the same as what I said about stories: that telling people what really happened might be boring unless you exaggerate some things and leave other things out. Which means you kind of have to lie to tell the truth.

Which is interesting to think about.

I think.

January 3rd

Okay, so here's the thing about Harold. He's not my real grandpa, who died when I was three, so I don't *have* to love him. But since he's my grandmother's boyfriend (it seems kind of bizarre to call a wrinkly old guy in his late seventies someone's "boyfriend"), it would be nice if at least I liked him. But I don't. Horrible Hairless Harold's impossible to like.

It's not because he looks like a turtle with his bald head peering up at you from under his hunched shoulders because you know me — I *love* animals. No, it's because after he shakes your hand he looks like he wants to rush to the bathroom to wash the germs off as fast as possible. And he's always correcting people's grammar — i.e., mine. Harold, old chap, I'm terribly sorry that I fail to live up to your expectations. But look at it this way: you need people like me to be superior to, don't you? We all can't be sanctimonious turtles with English accents.

"Sanctimonious turtles." That may be my favourite thing I've ever written, although obviously it has nothing to do with *real* turtles!

Maybe I'm delusional, but Harold's accent sounds fake to me, like he copied it from a movie and he's really an underworld mobster or a jewel thief from Bolivia planning a big heist. Boy, would my grandmother be mortified to find out that her

"Perfect Gentleman" was a crook in disguise! Enjoying this thought probably makes me a bad person but I can't help it; the guy really ticks me off.

(NOT **Harold**)

What irks me even more than Harold's accent, and the way he sniffs in disapproval whenever I use slang, is the way he treats Libby. He doesn't say hello to her when he comes into our house, he doesn't include her in conversation, and he never sits next to her. I don't think he even *looks* at her if he can avoid it.

A lot of people do that. Once they see a handicap — any kind of handicap — they don't know what to do. Vicky has an aunt who is blind, and she says that sometimes people talk to her too loudly or too slowly as if they assume that because she can't see them, she can't hear them either. But she has a much better attitude about the way people treat her than I do about the way they treat Libby. She thinks it's mostly ignorance rather than cruelty. So does my father, who says some of what I perceive as rudeness actually derives from sympathy. He thinks most people feel sad about Libby's situation and just don't know how to behave.

I don't agree with my dad. A lot of people don't act sympathetic at all. Some of them talk about Libby as though she's a *thing*, not a person, like that rude waitress where we went for brunch the last time we took Libby out to eat, sometime back in September. She asked my mother, "What will the girl in the wheelchair be having?" Before my mother could answer, I turned to Libby and asked in a loud voice, "Libby, would you like some fresh-squeezed orange juice?" and she opened her eyes wide, which means yes, so I said to the waitress, "My sister would like the orange juice please, with a straw. A bendy one, if possible." The waitress's face turned bright red, but I didn't care. She might have been ashamed for a nano-second, but I'll bet she'll be more polite the next time someone in a wheelchair rolls into her restaurant.

But I'm not allowed to confront Harold. My mother insists that I be nice to him "because Grandma loves him." All I can say is that if he really loves my grandmother, he should be making more of an effort to be nice to BOTH her granddaughters! He bought me a ticket to the ballet, but it doesn't take much effort to be nice to people who resemble you. It's much harder to be nice to people who are different.

And that concludes the ranting and raving portion of our programming for today.

In other news, Malcolm came back from his ski trip with a present for me! He gave me a box of water-colour pencils. How they work is that you draw with them and then go over the drawing with a wet paintbrush to change it into a painting. I felt bad that I didn't give him anything. It didn't occur to me that we'd be exchanging festive tokens of holiday cheer.

My own family isn't into the seasonal shopping frenzy and neither are my close friends, although we had a "Secret Santa" in homeroom, which means you pick a name out of a hat and buy that person a gift under $10. I got Louise Barnes, this girl who never talks, and because I had no clue what she would like I bought her a giant chocolate bar. Chocolate is a safe bet with most people, and she seemed to like it. I received a pair of blue knee-socks with little snowmen on them from my Santa, a guy with a beginner's moustache that looks like dirt on his upper lip, and I am quite smitten with them. In fact, I'm admiring them right now, although I'm suddenly feeling dubious because I just noticed that the snowmen are cuddling together under a branch of mistletoe.

I hope the socks aren't a coded message from that dude, because *yuck*.

Anyhow, besides the Secret Santa routine, the only person

outside my family I give presents to is Vicky, and I usually give her books. I offered to get Malcolm a book too, but he asked me to make a poster advertising his band for the school talent show instead. I'm worried about this project because frankly, manatees are not very inspiring. With those boneless bodies and saggy faces, they're kind of like the eggplants of the animal world.

(I may not be an eggplant, but my arms are definitely too short to play guitar with.)

(Not a manatee, but pretty darn close. Also unable to play the guitar.)

I'm going to look at a bunch of manatee photographs online and see if I can get inspired. Another approach might be to look through my father's record collection; he has a couple of boxes of vinyl down in the basement and some of the album covers have interesting designs on them. The talent show is next month and it may take me a while to figure out what to do, so I need to get started immediately.

As though I need another project! I'm getting nowhere trying to write a speech for my Bat Mitzvah, Mr. Davis. I can't understand why God punishes Miriam with leprosy (which is gross as well as potentially fatal; not only do your extremities rot but your nose gets eaten away — or it did back then, before they had the right drugs), but doesn't do anything at all to Aaron, who also criticizes Moses.

It doesn't make any *sense*. Isn't God supposed to be just and merciful as well as all-knowing? Not that God is, most of the time, in the bible, I admit it. But this is a more blatant example of injustice than most of them.

Okay, so here's the actual passage I have to discuss (well, it's not the only thing I have to discuss, but it's the part that interests me most): "And Miriam and Aaron spoke against Moses because of the Cushite woman whom he had married; for he had married a Cushite woman" (BeMidbar 12:1). "Cushite" is another name for Ethiopian, which means Moses' wife was Black (actually, she was his second wife and his first one was still alive, but that's another topic altogether).

At first I thought the point was that Aaron and Miriam were being prejudiced against Moses' new wife because she was a foreigner, or because she had dark skin, and that's why God was mad. Which meant I could have written a kickass speech about racism, something that I have strong feelings about. Except that God doesn't bother to defend the Cushite woman. God doesn't seem to care *why* Miriam and Aaron are complaining. God's just angry that they criticized Moses, the prophet, which means that they also disrespected Lord High Everything, Creator of the Universe, etcetera, etcetera.

And then, before going off in a huff, God strikes Miriam

with leprosy. ONLY Miriam. I know that she's the big sister and therefore expected to set a good example, but she and Aaron are already adults, so what's up with that? Is it because Miriam is a *woman* that she's not allowed to say anything? And why does Aaron pretend they have been punished equally, when he only gets yelled at and she gets a death sentence?

I know this is the bible, and in the bible women are almost never mentioned except as someone's mother or wife, but still. I have to write something that makes sense to me so that I can recite it in front of a room full of people and not feel like a total hypocrite when all I really want to say is, "Thank you for coming. Thank you for the book tokens. Enjoy your lunch because it cost my parents a lot of money. And remember to tell my grandmother how beautiful the flowers are, because she chose them herself."

February 10th

You know how I said that Moses' second wife was a Cushite woman, and therefore Black, and that if Aaron and Miriam had a problem with that, it would explain why God had a problem with them? And you know how I also said I didn't like my Grandmother Ruth's boyfriend Harold because he was a snob, and a phony, and rude to Libby? Well, it turns out not only is he rude, but Horrible Hairless Harold is *racist!*

And although I still don't know whether not there is an immortal being who created the universe and watches over it (if there is, they ought to be fired for doing a lousy job), and although I still don't know what such a being might feel about racists (because there sure seem to be a heck of a lot of them out there), I am very happy to report that my grandmother doesn't like them one little bit! In fact, my Grandma Ruth is a hero.

Here's what happened.

Last Thursday was the talent show at my school. Mum decided to come with me because she needed a night out and also because she likes Malcolm and wanted to hear him and his band perform. They were amazingly good! Not only is Malcolm awesome on guitar, which didn't surprise me given his family background, he also has a great voice, which I had no idea about. And it wasn't only me who thought so. Friday morning, the principal announced that *Manatee Patrol* was voted the best band at the talent show. Everybody was allowed to drop a ballot in a box as they were leaving, so I made Mum vote even though she wasn't sure she should since she was technically not a student at the school. But the voting was for *audience* favourite, not for *student* favourite, so I'm sure that was legit.

Anyhow, when we got home we told Dad and Libby all about the talent show and Libby paid attention for once, so we asked her if she'd like to hear Malcolm play his guitar and she opened her eyes wide, which means "yes." So I asked him if he would mind giving a little private performance sometime, and he came over on the weekend and serenaded her.

My grandmother happened to be visiting and she asked Malcolm if he could play some Bach for her and he whipped off a classical piece on the spot without a single mistake. Naturally, she was impressed. Then she asked him all sorts of old-lady questions about whether he hoped to have a career as a musician (he doesn't) and what he wants to do instead (he wants to be a doctor in Haiti, where his mother came from, because they need better medical care there). When Harold came over to pick her up to go out to dinner she introduced Malcolm to him, and Harold gave him the usual dead-fish handshake except even more reluctantly than usual. Then, after Malcolm went home, Grandma Ruth couldn't stop talking about what a lovely young man he was, and what beautiful manners he had, and so on, until Harold said sharply that he didn't think I should associate with somebody like that.

Grandma said, "What on earth do you mean, Harold? Someone like what?" and Harold said, "That boy has Negro blood, Ruth. Can't you tell?" And my grandma narrowed her eyes at him and said, in a voice that could wither a cactus, "Well, perhaps he shouldn't associate with somebody like Sophie, since her blood is Jewish. Can't you tell?"

He was stunned. He kept insisting that that was different. And she said no, Harold, it's exactly the same, and if you can't see that, you are not the man I thought you were. Finally, he apologized. He said he was sorry if he misspoke because who her granddaughter was friends with was none of his business, but she didn't let him off the hook. Grandma just said, "Enough. We don't associate with racists in this family. So goodbye, Harold. I never want to see you again," and she walked over clickety-clack in her high-heeled patent-leather sling-backed shoes, opened the front door, and shooed him out like he was a stray cat.

And that was the end of Harold!

Before Harold got the boot, I had always assumed my Grandma Ruth was stuck-up like him because she insists on good grooming and proper manners. I thought she was judging everybody else — especially me — and that we all disappointed her. But I was totally wrong.

She burst into tears after Harold left and started talking about her childhood, and how she was born in a displaced persons camp, and how both her parents lost the rest of their families in the Holocaust. She even told us some of the terrible things people said about them when they first immigrated here … the kind of stuff we never talk about in this house because it's painful and it happened long ago. She said that she had promised herself that her children and grandchildren would never be made to feel unworthy the way she had, and that she would never make anyone *else* feel that way either. She said that she was ashamed a man she spent so much time with could spew that kind of poison and she hoped we would forgive her for exposing us to him.

Her mascara was running down her face, which was weird since she's always immaculate. My mother started hugging her and telling her she was a wonderful mother and grandmother and that she wasn't responsible in any way for Harold's behaviour. I stood there feeling guilty for being sassy about my grandma all the time. Old people seem like they've always been old, don't they, and since nobody ever told me anything about her childhood, it hadn't occurred to me to ask about it. Which was selfish.

So I started crying too.

And then, since they didn't need me and I didn't want to get noticed, I snuck into Libby's room and updated her about what had just happened in case she hadn't been listening, which was a safe bet given how she's been behaving lately, i.e., Not In This World. And then we watched *Ladyhawke* for a while until things got back to normal — or as close to normal as they ever get at my house.

THE DISCOVERY OF FLIGHT
by Elizabeth Adler

CHAPTER THIRTEEN

At the end of the first day on the road, the scavengers unhitch their weary horses from the wagon to let them nibble the dusty autumn grass. The path they have been following runs along the river and Adam wants to jump in for a swim but no one else is interested in getting wet. So he busies himself gathering sticks and bark and building a fire, letting out little whoops of pleasure as the flames catch and sparks fly up into the starlit sky. He dances crazily around the fire chanting nonsense until the others join him, waving their arms and shaking their hips, laughing until they cry.

Like Adam, Terra has never been away from her parents before, but unlike him, she is nervous about the separation rather than exuberant. Once they sit down to heat water for tea and eat their meager rations of bread, cheese, and apples, she admits some of her fears.

"Should we be worried about wild animals out here? Did you run into any wolves or bears on your previous trips?"

"No," replies the older girl, Laurel. "Although one night, something spooked the horses."

"What did you do?"

"We made torches, hoping that we could use them to chase whatever it was away. Luckily, it never came back."

"I think that we should take turns standing guard," says Adam.

"But we're supposed to do everything in pairs," Terra objects. "That's the rule." After all, she can't tell the others they have nothing to worry about because a sharp-eyed hawk will be watching over them all night long, and that the hawk will tell her if there is any prospect of danger. Besides, she isn't entirely sure that is true, not having heard from Aya for hours. Is she nearby? Is she still listening to Terra's thoughts?

"If we work in pairs, we will only get to sleep half the night and nobody will be rested tomorrow," Adam replies.

"I agree with Adam," says the other boy, Sol. "Anyhow, I don't see any Elders around here, do you? We can make up our *own* minds for a change."

"Don't be too overconfident, Sol," Laurel says, "or you may not live to be an Elder yourself."

"Right now, I'm more concerned about living until tomorrow morning. How good are you with a bow and arrow, Adam?"

"Not as good as you are, but good enough. I also have a dagger; I am better at hand-to-hand combat."

"My father taught me how to throw a knife from a distance, so hopefully we can avoid hand-to-hand combat." Terra isn't even sure she has made this remark aloud because she suddenly hears Aya's voice in her head: *Don't worry, my sister; I will protect your mate.*

Adam is not my "mate," Terra thinks back at her, indignantly.

You can't hide your feelings from me, Terra. You aren't worried about the other humans the way you are about him.

I don't know them as well as I know him, Aya; that's all.

As you wish, the hawk replies. *Meanwhile, you should rest while your "not-mate" and I stand guard.*

Don't you need to sleep too? Terra asks.

I can rest with one eye open. And even if I doze off, I will wake if anything comes this way.

"Terra," Laurel says, sounding irritated. "Please pay attention."

"What?"

"We're having an important discussion and need your input."

"Sorry."

"We're trying to decide whether to sleep in the wagon or nearer to the fire on the bare ground."

"I don't care," Terra replies.

"I vote for the wagon," says Sol. "If we stay close together our body heat will keep us warm."

"But shouldn't we keep the fire going all night to chase away predators?"

"Well, whoever is keeping watch can sit beside the fire and keep feeding it," Adam proposes. "Then we can have the best of both worlds."

"That makes sense," Laurel agrees. "Meanwhile the rest of us should go to sleep so someone else can relieve Adam in a couple of hours."

"Who will that be?" asks Sol.

"Adam comes first alphabetically so I'll go next, then you, Sol, and Terra last," Laurel replies, the tidiness of this system consoling her for this unprecedented departure from the Elders' rules.

The night goes off without a hitch and the next morning they continue their journey as a real team. Terra has never spent this much time with people her own age before and feels a new light-heartedness, as well as a certain recklessness, overtaking her. She is glad they have three more days together without any parents or teachers or Elders telling them what to do; very glad to be away from the noise and fuss and lack of privacy at home.

"This is weird," she observes aloud. "Even though we're travelling in a group, I feel like I'm alone for the first time in my life."

"Me too," Adam agrees. "Because for once I'm not defined by my family."

"Exactly! It's as though I'm finally thinking my own thoughts without worrying whether they're the right ones. For example, last night, when you boiled those eggs for supper, I suddenly realized that I hate runny eggs even though that's the way my mother always makes them."

"You never noticed that before?" Adam is amazed.

"Oh, I noticed," Terra laughs. "But it didn't occur to me to question the way things were done at home. I just put up with them."

"What an obedient child you are, little Terra."

"I tend to avoid conflict so that people will leave me alone."

"Does that work?" he asks dubiously. "I mean, don't they just keep imposing their will on you because you never say no?"

"Well, sometimes I do what they ask and other times I ... disappear. Go for a walk or something to get out of the line of fire. I can't stand fighting."

"Why?"

"Maybe because my older sister used to argue with my parents all the time and it never changed anything; she still thought *she* was right and they still thought *they* were right. And I could see that both sides had a point, which made me tired and confused."

"Why do people waste their lives fussing over things that aren't important?" Adam sighs.

"Well, how do *you* think we should live our lives?"

"Exactly as we are at this moment," he replies, with surprising enthusiasm.

"As we are at this moment? You mean in the back of a wagon behind two of the world's laziest horses?"

"No, I mean like we might die tomorrow, so we don't have any regrets about what we missed out on."

"But if I died tomorrow I would have missed out on my whole life!" Terra objects. "I wouldn't have married, or had children, or lived in my own house. I wouldn't even have learned how to be a decent artist."

"Good," says Adam, putting his arm around Terra again, and pulling her closer towards him.

"What's good?" she asks, feeling the pounding of his heart through his thin cotton shirt. Or maybe it is her own heart, speeding up.

"Now that you know what you want to do with your life, make sure you don't let anyone stop you from doing it."

And then he kisses her.

Just friends, eh? Aya would have been laughing, if hawks were able to laugh.

Malcolm gave me a valentine. Vicky says that means we are officially "going out," although I reminded her that I would be the first to know if I were dating somebody, particularly somebody as hot as Malcolm West, who a lot of the girls in our grade have crushes on. I was joking when I said that, but Vicky was serious. She kept arguing that these days, boys don't ask you out for a soda or take you to the sock-hop like they do in the old *Archie* comics she inherited from an older cousin. Boys today decide that you're the one they like without necessarily telling you so; you are expected to be able read their signals through the static caused by large groups of adolescents doing everything together. Including a lot of flirting, and hugging, and hanging out trying to look cool in case anyone notices.

Vicky added that high school students are just like a bunch of chimpanzees grooming each other.

Are you implying that I have lice, or that Malcolm does? I asked her, trying to keep the conversation light. Vicky is obsessed with evolutionary biology — which is when you study animals to find out why people act the way they do — and I could tell that she was getting ready to give me a lecture on primate behaviour. Since I'd heard that lecture a few times before, the only way I could stop her was to admit that I do like Malcolm and would not be displeased to find out that we were, in fact, dating, if that were, in fact, the case.

Which it isn't.

All we ever do is talk and listen to music and eat whatever snacks my mother makes for us, including her failed experiments (falling-apart falafel; lumpy crème caramel). A lot of the time we do these things in Libby's room, trying to make her feel included. It's true that my sister is not the most vigilant chaperone on the planet but still, Malcolm's never even tried to kiss me. He has put his arm around me a couple of times, but I'm not sure that counts. (I can't believe I wrote that where my teacher can read it! Now you know more about me than you probably want to, Mr. Davis. Although when I think about how boy-crazy some of the other girls in our Hebrew class are, I kind of doubt it.)

Anyhow, Malcolm knows a ton of Indie bands I've never heard of and also — which is not surprising given that his dad is a jazz musician — he's a huge fan of old-school jazz and blues. After all, if we can read books by dead authors and enjoy them, why shouldn't we enjoy listening to dead musicians? He made me a mix-tape and there's this one song, "Feeling Good," that gives me the chills. He says it was his mother's favourite song and he thinks about her every time he listens to it.

I understand why. The singer, Nina Simone, sounds terribly sad, despite the fact that the words to the song look completely happy on the page. She sings like her heart has been broken, and she's wandering around looking at birds flying to convince herself that everything will be all right because nature goes on being beautiful no matter how much tragedy there is. Which I totally get. And that Malcolm gets it too is one of the reasons we've become so close.

Whether or not we're actually "dating."

February 27th

I talked to Grandma Ruth about my Bat Mitzvah speech. First I asked her whether she thought I should focus on racism, now that I know that's an issue she cares about. Although she agreed that it is important to combat racism, she didn't think the topic was central to the text. But because she could see that I was frustrated and she knows that I usually don't have a hard time saying what I think, she asked me to explain what the problem was. And talking to her helped me figure out what I want to say!

This is a huge relief, because I was beginning to worry that I might have to stand there in the fancy new dress and shoes Grandma bought me and do magic tricks to distract the congregation (although Vicky says that watching me try to walk in high heels is entertainment enough). Really, I had absolutely no idea what to say. Zip. *Nada.* Or, as my father would say, "a great big goose egg."

But now I feel like my head is on fire, so I'm going to write down everything I'm thinking while it's still fresh. Before The Big Day I can always stick in quotations from the bible or the occasional Hebrew word so that I sound learned and sincere. I will copy it in here when it's finished.

THE DISCOVERY OF FLIGHT
by Elizabeth Adler

CHAPTER FOURTEEN

They arrive at their destination before nightfall. Formerly neat cottages and gardens and sprucely fenced fields have been transformed into a jagged mess of shattered walls, charred trees, and mud. Although the smell of smoke has dissipated in the months since the attack, the village remains colourless and grim and, in the dusk, eerily silent: a habitation fit only for ghosts.

Terra starts to cry, picking her way through the rubble in the direction of what used to be her family home.

"Wait, Terra!" Laurel shouts. "Don't wander off on your own. It's going to get dark soon."

"We aren't going to be able to get any work done tonight, are we?" asks Sol.

"No, but..."

"Then let the poor kid check out her house. I'll bet Adam wants to do the same thing. Those two haven't been back here before and you know how shocking it is at first. I'll go build a fire at the old mill; we can sleep there tonight."

"We'll meet you there in half an hour, okay?" Adam asks.

"Okay."

Terra doesn't say a word, overcome at the enormity of the disaster all around them. Rationally, of course, she had expected this. She'd walked through the smouldering remains of the place as they'd fled, she'd heard the reports of previous teams of scavengers and seen the pathetic junk they'd retrieved from the wreckage, she'd spent countless weary hours helping to rebuild another village that had received exactly the same treatment as this one. She had inhaled its stink and sifted through its debris, her hands torn and full of splinters, her heart heavy. How, despite the evidence of her senses, had the fantasy persisted that her own home would still be standing?

The door to her house swings open, a gateway into emptiness, and she walks through. Of the four original walls only part of the rear one remains, braced by the stone fireplace with its massive hearth. With trembling hands, Terra pulls out a big pink hearthstone veined with sparkling quartz. She finds her sketchbook wedged between it and the next block, completely untouched.

"What's that?"

Terra turns to find Adam right behind her.

"My sketchbook."

"Why didn't it get burned up in the fire?"

"I always put it between these two stones to press the pages flat, and the stones must have protected it."

"Is that why you asked to come along on this trip? Because you wanted to find your sketchbook?"

"Yes. Maybe that's selfish but I really need it."

"It's not selfish at all," Adam says, taking the book from her and flipping through the pages, stopping now and again at an image that catches his attention. On one page an Elder drowses in the summer sun, his gnarled fingers clutching his staff as though they themselves have been carved out of wood; on another, a gleaming copper pot holds a bunch of yellow flowers and feathery green leaves; a third displays a brown moth spreading its delicate wings against rugged bark that almost camouflages it completely.

"These are great, Terra! You are an amazing artist. I wish I had talent like you do."

"Everybody has talents, Adam. Maybe you haven't found yours yet."

"Maybe."

"What are you good at?"

"I'm pretty good at playing music. I'm also good with animals. I've trained my dog Shadow very well and my uncle always asks me to help him at lambing time. But I don't want to be a shepherd for the rest of my life."

"I'm sure there are other things you can do involving animals. They are a lot smarter than most people think. Maybe you could learn how to communicate with them."

Thanks for that, says a voice in her head.

I didn't know you were here, Aya, Terra thinks back, trying to hide her surprise from Adam.

I will not leave you on this journey, my sister.

"Terra?"

"Yes?"

"We should go back to the others now, if you're ready. "

"Okay, I'm coming." And taking one last look about her, silently saying goodbye to her childhood, Terra follows Adam out into the ruined village.

Laurel and Sol have built a fire outside the mill and are making soup with some scraps of dried meat and a handful of beans and peas.

"Are you hungry?" Laurel asks.

"I'm always hungry!" Adam replies. "But that doesn't look very … substantial."

"Well, if you want to go see if there's anything edible left in the fields, be my guest."

"I'll go with him," says Sol, eagerly.

"What can I do to help?" Terra asks.

"Maybe you could check out the mill to make sure it's still safe to sleep there."

Terra is sweeping away pebbles and dirt with an improvised broom made of twigs when she suddenly hears noises coming from a far corner. They are weak cries, not growls of aggression, so she takes a deep breath and walks over to the place they are coming from. Startling green eyes stare up at her from a pile of straw where a scrawny grey cat lies. Terra can make out the tip of its tail twitching in the gloom.

"Don't be afraid, Kitty."

The cat doesn't move. It just keeps staring at her. Its mouth isn't moving either but faint mewing sounds can still be heard. Terra finally realizes that the cat is nursing six tiny kittens.

"What a good mama you are!" she says. "You should come back with us; I know lots of people who would love to give you and your babies new homes." And she runs out of the mill to fetch a cup of water for the mother cat, who laps it up quickly with her neat pink tongue and then licks Terra's hand in gratitude.

Mmmmm, says a voice in her head. *Those look tasty.*

Humans don't eat cats, Aya!

Well, you should. In fact, I was going to suggest that you drop a couple into that mess the other girl is cooking.

No way. I'm bringing them home for all the children who lost their pets when we ran away from here.

You don't know what you're missing.

Meanwhile Adam and Sol have returned with a couple of onions, some overgrown whiskery carrots, and three potatoes, all of which are quickly peeled, chopped up, and thrown into the bubbling pot.

"We've already done a great job of scavenging even though we weren't supposed to start work until tomorrow. So far we've collected a cat, six kittens, and some vegetables," Laurel laughs, as they spoon up the soup.

"Aren't you going to show them your sketchbook?" Adam whispers to Terra.

"Maybe later," she whispers back. "Let's see what else we find tomorrow."

THE DISCOVERY OF FLIGHT
by Elizabeth Adler

CHAPTER FIFTEEN

The next morning is much colder than the previous one. Although the four scavengers put on every garment they have, they still shiver in the wind that blows through the ruined village, throwing dust in their faces and making their work more miserable than they had anticipated. By lunchtime, however, when they meet outside the mill to brew hot tea and gnaw on stale bread and cheese, they are heartened to discover how many useful items they have managed to retrieve. Sol has scored the best prize: an axe, still sharp and in excellent condition, stuck in a tree stump beyond the far field. It has taken him a long time to work it free so he has little else to offer but a coil of fraying rope, but they all recognize that the axe's value outweighs that of anything the rest of them have found: Laurel's milking stool and accompanying pail, chipped clay urn, and dirty hair comb; Adam's sewing needles, thimble, handful of bone buttons, three spools of thread, and jar of brackish vinegar; Terra's leather belt, tin pan, child-sized spoon, and wooden flute.

After lunch, they decide to concentrate on what might still be waiting for them out in the fields. And by the time darkness falls they have accumulated a lot more carrots and potatoes as well as some turnips and several gargantuan cabbages.

"Not a bad day's work. My mum will be thrilled when she sees these potatoes."

"Whatever we bring back belongs to the whole community, not to a single family, Adam," Laurel reminds him primly.

"I know, I know," he replies mildly, showing far less irritation than Terra would have. "But my mother's potato pancakes are the food of the gods. In fact, you're all invited back to my house for dinner when we get home."

"It's so weird to hear you call our new place 'home,'" Terra sighs. "Especially when we are sitting in the place where we grew up."

"I was thinking the same thing," Sol adds.

"Really?" says Adam. "To me, home isn't a place; it's the people you live with. The people you come back to after you go somewhere else."

"When have you ever gone away?" Sol asks. "Before this, I mean."

"Never. But I've always been restless, and this trip has taught me how much I like being on the move. I don't want to spend the rest of my life stuck in one spot."

"Where do you want to go?" Laurel inquires, uncharacteristically curious.

"I have no idea. Anywhere. Everywhere."

"Doesn't the idea of wandering around strange places by yourself scare you?"

"Who says I'd be alone?" Adam replies, sneaking a glance at Terra. Luckily the others don't notice her blushing in the dark.

"I can't think that far ahead." Sol yawns. "In fact, all I can think about right now is S-L-E-E-P. Are you willing to take the first watch again, Adam?"

"Sure. You guys go to bed. I'm going to sit by the fire and imagine my future. Climbing mountains, sailing rivers — there's a big world out there and I want to see it!" Adam stands up and stretches his arms as wide as he can, as if to embrace all the possibilities life holds for him.

Terra wishes she had some of his enthusiasm but she is so exhausted that sleep overcomes her as soon as she lies down. She can't help groaning when Sol pokes her in the ribs what seems like a few minutes later, signaling that it is her turn to sit by the fire.

"I'm so sore," she moans. "It feels like I broke every bone in my body."

"You'll feel better once you get moving," he reassures her.

"Do you really think there is much more we can do around here?"

"Well, there are a few houses and outbuildings we haven't gone through yet, and we still have to check to see if there's anything left in the orchards. Also, we had special instructions to bring back fence-posts and timbers to enclose the new village. So we probably won't go home until tomorrow morning."

"*Home.* You said it too, Sol."

"I know."

Ms. Sophie Adler's Extremely Personal Bat Mitzvah Speech

You all know the story of the Israelites escaping from Egypt and wandering in the desert for forty years, but you may not be familiar with the particular incident related in my Torah portion; an incident I myself had a lot of trouble understanding. In fact, I had so much trouble with it that I kept wishing I had been assigned the plague of frogs or the parting of the Red Sea. The miraculous stuff that happens earlier in Exodus seemed much more exciting than what I was supposed to talk about today. To sum it up, in my portion, Aaron and Miriam criticize Moses, who might be a mighty prophet to the rest of the Israelites but is still their little brother. As a result, God punishes Miriam with leprosy and, because leprosy is contagious, she is sent into exile in the desert, away from the Israeli camp. Only after Moses pleads with God to forgive her is she cured and allowed to come home.

No matter how much I thought about this story, it never made any sense to me. The first problem was that it seemed to be saying that God is unjust, punishing Miriam with leprosy for criticizing Moses but doing nothing to Aaron, who was equally guilty. Unless you believe — as some ancient rabbis apparently did — that Aaron's punishment was that he was made to feel guilty that his sister suffered a terrible illness but he did not.

Well, as everyone here knows, I have experienced that exact same situation. My sister suffers from a terrible illness and I don't. And yes, I feel guilty that I am the healthy one. But the idea that God punished Miriam as a way of punishing *Aaron* still doesn't make sense to me, because the Torah is supposed to be a guide for how to live a good and useful life. And what's the lesson here? "Don't do bad stuff or your sister will be punished."

This not only makes no sense. It's evil.

The second thing that bothered me is that God tells Miriam and Aaron they should have *known* they weren't allowed to criticize their brother, because criticizing Moses was the same as criticizing God. This version of God isn't evil; it's more like a bad teacher who puts stuff that was never taught to you on a test.

The more I thought about my Torah portion, and the more I discussed it with my Grandma Ruth, who helped me a lot with this speech, the more it seemed to me that the idea of God punishing Miriam was *superstition*, not religion. The superstition of frightened people who needed an explanation for why bad things happen. I started to suspect that what really occurred was something much simpler, like Miriam getting an infection from wandering around in the desert without any soap or water or medical care. I'll spare you the results of my internet research about skin diseases, because some of the photos were gross, but "white scales" — which is how Miriam's disease is described — sounds a lot more like eczema or psoriasis than it does like leprosy. She could even have gotten white scales from a bad sunburn, which would be easy to get in the desert.

However, not having access to Google, the ancient Israelites jumped to the conclusion that she had *leprosy*. And once they made that diagnosis, it seemed to them that she must have done something very bad to deserve such a terrible fate. But since Miriam hadn't committed any obvious crimes, the only bad thing they could think of was her criticism of her brother Moses. So *that* became the reason she got leprosy.

The only problem with their diagnosis was that her skin cleared up a week later. This doesn't happen with leprosy. If you have leprosy, you get sicker and sicker until your nose rots away and your fingers and toes fall off. But instead of reaching the logical conclusion — that Miriam never had leprosy in the first place — the Israelites decided that the same God who had punished her before had now forgiven her.

In other words, frightened people, wandering in a desert, tried to make random events meaningful by saying God caused them. They couldn't admit that sometimes God isn't involved in what happens to us. Sometimes there is nothing but good or bad LUCK.

Only bad luck can explain the situation of people like my sister Libby, who was *born* sick and therefore couldn't have done anything she "deserved" to be punished for. Cerebral palsy isn't even contagious, but plenty of people don't want to look at Libby or even talk to her because they're worried they'll catch what she has, the same way the ancient Israelites were afraid they'd catch leprosy from Miriam. And like the ancient Israelites, they seem to need to find someone or something to blame. My parents' DNA. The doctor who delivered Libby. The pesticides in our food; the fluoride in our water, the antibiotics my mum took for bronchitis. Cell phones. Microwave ovens. Gluten.

There's no point repeating all the stupid things people have said over the years about my sister's condition, sometimes when she could hear them, because today is supposed to be a day of celebration. But what I've learned from thinking about Miriam's disease, whatever it was, and relating it to my own experience of living with my sister Libby, is that healthy people don't want to face their fear of illness, so they turn their backs on sick people in two ways. Number 1) They blame them for getting sick, and Number 2) They exile them by putting them into special schools, or refusing to look at them, or talking about them as though they aren't present.

But as my brilliant Grandmother Ruth pointed out to me, these two reactions contradict each other! Think about it for a minute. If the ancient Israelites really believed that Miriam was being punished by God, why would they have been afraid that she was contagious? You can't catch someone else's punishment! By sending her into exile, they were *admitting* that they knew she was suffering from an ordinary disease, and not from something supernatural.

Well, the Israelites might not have known what kind of skin condition Miriam had or how she got it, but today we know a lot more than they do, even if we can't cure everything yet. So there is no excuse for superstition around sick or disabled people. We should know by now that we are not BETTER than them because we are healthy. We are just LUCKIER.

(I know I need to write a better conclusion and stop shouting, Mr. Davis, but I am so happy I finally wrote something that makes sense!

THE DISCOVERY OF FLIGHT
by Elizabeth Adler

CHAPTER SIXTEEN

The third morning, Sol and Laurel go to the orchard to pick whatever fruit still hangs on the trees, uneaten by birds or beasts. Adam and Terra scavenge through the buildings the group has not yet combed through. All four of them plan to work together after lunch, pulling up fence posts for the palisade around their new village.

"It may sound callous, but I'm kind of enjoying this," Terra says to Adam, as they stumble over fallen timbers and scattered bricks.

"I know. It's like going on a treasure hunt, only you don't have a map and you don't know what the treasure is going to be," he agrees.

"Not knowing what you are going to discover is half the fun! I was so excited to find that flute."

"Do you think the Elders will let me keep it?" Adam asks, a yearning note in his voice Terra has not heard there before.

"I forgot that you were good at music, Adam. Will you play something for us tonight?"

"Laurel probably won't give her permission. She'll just repeat that everything we find belongs to the whole village, etcetera, etcetera."

"I'm sure she won't mind if you play the flute now as long as we give it to the Elders when we get back."

"You're probably right, but I swear, sometimes I want to punch her."

They are still laughing when Terra spies something glittering under a pile of rubble behind one of the stables. She runs over and starts to dig it up with her bare hands but it is buried too deep to dislodge easily. Adam moves some bricks and stones out of the way and then together they lever it out of the dirt using a long branch.

To their delight, it is a plow, still in good working order.

"Ha!" Adam exclaims, throwing his arms around Terra and giving her a big hug. "Wait until the Elders see this! They will be thrilled. I am definitely getting my flute."

"Let's move the rest of this debris, Adam, in case there's more farm equipment stuck underneath it," Terra suggests.

It takes them at least thirty minutes to shift the pile but their effort yields a rake, a hoe, two leather straps, at least twenty rusty nails, and the remains of a wooden bucket.

"This really *is* a treasure chest, Terra! Let's go see if there's any more booty inside the stable."

Adam takes off without waiting. A couple of minutes later Terra finds him kneeling inside the broken-down structure, his hand resting on the skeleton of what looks like a foal. It lies, its skinny legs tucked under its narrow rib-cage, beside the remains of two mature horses and some smaller creature, probably a goat. Most of their flesh has rotted or been gnawed away but there are still some scraps of hide and hair covering their bones. The smell of decay persists about the place despite all the time that has passed, but that doesn't seem to bother Adam. He just keeps stroking the pony's sightless forehead as tears run down his cheek.

Terra starts to cry too.

"This is awful. I thought all our animals got away safely. Nobody told us they found corpses in the stables."

"I guess these guys were tied up when the fire started," Adam says softly.

"This little filly wasn't even weaned yet. I was there when she was born, Terra. She was so pretty — black with a white blaze and white stockings. How could those monsters kill innocent animals? It makes me hate them even more."

I like this boy, Aya's voice ripples through Terra's thoughts. *He has a kind heart.*

Yes, Terra thinks back. *And even though you startled me, I'm glad you are here. Because now I'm scared.*

These were not the only animals killed by the Invaders, Terra. Some escaped to the woods where they died alone and in pain. And before they attacked your village, they had already murdered countless birds for the sake of their feathers.

I had forgotten that, Aya. I am truly sorry.

Hawks do not forget anything, my sister. So if the time ever comes that we must fight, I will be able to raise an army to help us.

That is good to know.

Maybe because they are so upset by the sight in the stable, Terra and Adam discover little else of value, just some moth-eaten cloth, a pair of children's sandals, and a plate. And when they meet the others for lunch, they display what they have found with less exultation than anticipated.

"This is so great, Adam!" says Sol. "Where did you find all the farm equipment?"

"Behind the little stable."

"Huh. I never thought of going over there; it was pretty much burned to the ground, wasn't it?"

"It wasn't the only thing," Adam replied grimly.

"What do you mean?" asks Laurel.

"There were four animals inside who didn't escape the fire. One of them was a brand new foal."

It turns out that neither of the others knew about the dead animals, though surely one of the previous expeditions had stumbled upon them. Apparently, a decision had been made, probably by the Elders, to suppress the information.

"I wonder what else they aren't telling us?" Sol asks, indignantly. "If they want us to risk our lives by coming here, you'd think they'd inform us honestly about what to expect!"

"I'm sure it was for our own good. They wanted to keep us from panicking."

"You *would* say that, Laurel."

"Adam, be polite. We need each other more than ever," Terra interjects, finally entering the discussion.

"What do you mean?" asks Adam.

"We can't keep pretending we're just having an adventure. We always knew there was the possibility of real danger here."

"Terra's right," says Laurel, holding a slim hand out to each of the boys. "Shake, and let's be friends. If we do a good job this afternoon, we can leave first thing tomorrow."

Adam and Sol shake hands with Laurel, feeling ashamed of themselves. And after an inadequate lunch of boiled cabbage followed by withered apples from the orchard, everyone goes back to work side by side, in silence. The smell of death — a smell they had somehow allowed themselves to forget — is now in their nostrils, so they work as fast as they can, eager to leave. Ignoring their fatigue and hunger, they pull up fence posts that have been hammered deep into the earth and dismantle wooden structures nail by nail.

And when Adam asks if he can play the flute, Laurel doesn't object. The music rises up silver as starlight; it rises up to the sky like a prayer.

THE DISCOVERY OF FLIGHT
by Elizabeth Adler

CHAPTER SEVENTEEN

When morning comes they load the household furnishings, tools, farm equipment, and a load of splintery wood into the wagon, and fill two wheelbarrows with fruits and vegetables. It is lucky that the horses are well rested, because the wagon is a lot heavier on the return trip than it was on the way down. And now that there is no room for passengers, they have to take turns riding up front and pushing the wheelbarrows behind. Unlike the horses, they are tired and cold, covered with cuts and bruises, their muscles sore and their bellies hungry, but they forge ahead as best they can, hardly talking.

The winding path along the river no longer seems as easy to follow nor the surrounding woods as friendly as when they'd set out. They find themselves startling every time they hear a noise. Once night falls and they are huddled around the smallest of campfires, worried that the smoke might draw the wrong kind of attention but too cold to do without it, Terra asks Adam to play the flute again, hoping that it will cheer them up.

"We should keep quiet tonight, I think," he says.

"I agree," said Laurel, cuddling one of the kittens and looking less sure of herself than usual. Following her example, each of them takes a kitten to bed, the small warm bodies providing comfort and reassurance that they will reach home safely.

They are still a couple of hours from their destination the following day when Aya appears above the treetops, screeching urgently. Terra stops pushing her wheelbarrow, the blood turning to ice in her veins.

"Do you have a cramp in your leg?" asks Laurel, trudging along beside her.

"No," Terra replies. "But please be quiet. I have to listen."

"Listen to what?" Laurel asks, confused. "I don't hear anything."

Terra ignores her because the hawk's voice is filling her mind and blocking out everything else.

The evil ones are returning, my sister. Shay saw them headed in the direction of your village, carrying weapons.

Can we get home in time to warn everyone?

He thinks so.

Good. Except that I don't know how I'm going to explain this. No one will believe me.

Adam will believe you.

"Terra!" Laurel is shaking her, her face panicky. "Are you all right?"

"Yes, sorry. But we need to talk. It's an emergency, Laurel. Go get the others, okay?"

Laurel drops the handles of her wheelbarrow and runs ahead to tell the boys that something strange has happened to Terra, who is standing in the middle of the path and refusing to move. Adam jumps down from the wagon without waiting for Sol, who stops to tie the reins to a sturdy branch before following the others back. They find Terra where Laurel left her, staring at something directly above her. Two magnificent red-tailed hawks are perched on a leafless oak, the tree itself scarred by lightning but still standing tall against the deeper green of the surrounding pines and spruces. To their surprise, the birds do not fly away at their approach but only glance briefly in their direction and then fix their golden eyes back on the motionless girl.

"Terra?" asks Adam, tentatively. "Are you okay?"

"Yes, but we are in grave danger."

"From the hawks? Don't worry; they only eat small animals like mice. You're completely safe."

Terra can't help laughing despite the gravity of the situation. "The hawks aren't the danger. They came to help us."

"Terra, I think you need to rest," says Sol, exchanging a worried look with Laurel, who nods. "In fact, we can all use a break. How about if I go get some fresh water?"

They think I've gone crazy, Terra realizes. At this, both hawks flap their wings and screech.

"No, no, there's no time to waste! We must hurry back to the Elders to warn them," she replies, sounding as frantic as the birds.

"Warn them about what?" asks Adam.

"The Invaders are moving in the direction of the new village."

"How do you know?"

"I told you, Adam; the hawks came to warn us."

"You can speak to hawks?"

"Yes."

"She's hallucinating. I *told* you something was wrong with her," said Laurel.

"I am perfectly well," Terra retorts indignantly.

"I believe you, Terra," Adam says.

"Aya said you would."

"Who is Aya?"

"The bigger hawk; the female," Terra replies, pointing. To Adam's amazement, the larger of the two hawks bows her head as if acknowledging the introduction.

"How do you do, Lady Aya?" he finds himself saying, and bows back.

Your mate has nice manners, the hawk thinks to the girl.

"This is ridiculous!" Sol shouts, stamping his foot with frustration. "We are standing in the woods pretending to talk to birds!"

Why is that boy screeching? Aya asks.

He doesn't believe me. Laurel doesn't either; I can tell by her face.

I think we need to give them a demonstration.

How?

Don't ask me, my sister; I've never understood humans.

"I can prove that I can talk to them," Terra says, feeling less resolute than she sounds.

"How?" Sol inquires skeptically.

"Maybe if you tell me what you want, I can ask them to get it for you. Would that convince you?"

"Sure; fine. I would love a cup of tea. And a cookie would be nice too."

"No, seriously. Something they can find nearby."

"How about a flower?" asks Laurel, surprising everyone, including herself. "Or even two flowers? Perhaps Aya can find a yellow one and the other hawk can get a purple one."

"His name is Shay," Terra says, feeling that she'd been rude, not introducing him. "But yes, that will be perfect."

And before she has finished speaking, the hawks have vanished. They return a few minutes later, Aya with some faded yellow yarrow hanging from her beak. She drops the flower at Laurel's feet, then flies back to the oak tree and begins to preen herself nonchalantly. Shay circles the group with a clump of asters wrenched out of the earth, roots and all, before letting it fall a short distance away, concerned that he might spray everyone with dirt. Then he too joins Aya and waits for the humans to respond.

They are speechless. Except for Terra.

Your mate has nice manners too, she tells Aya.

THE DISCOVERY OF FLIGHT
by Elizabeth Adler

CHAPTER EIGHTEEN

Laurel picks up the stalk of yarrow and twirls it around in her fingers. She stares at it, astonished, before speaking. "Since I'm the one responsible for this expedition, I need to go ahead with Terra to explain to the Elders that the village is in danger. Sol, Adam — you two follow with the wheelbarrows as quickly as you can."

"We could run much faster if we left them behind," Adam says.

"It doesn't make sense to abandon the food we've gathered," Sol retorts. "We'll need it, especially if we're going to have to fight."

"Sol's right," Terra agrees, as the hawks fly off ahead of them.

Laurel urges the reluctant horses to trot. They are surprised to have to increase the leisurely pace at which they've been travelling. When they finally reach the outskirts of the village, they hear a series of hooting noises: sentries in the trees signaling that friends have arrived.

Humans don't make very convincing owls, Aya remarks.

Well, maybe you can give us lessons, Terra replies.

And then the Elders come to meet them.

"Why are you making those poor horses work so hard? And where are the boys?" asks a stern-looking woman.

"You promised that you would all stay together, Laurel," adds a man with a long grey beard.

"I apologize for not following your instructions, Venerable Ones," Laurel replies, bowing. "The boys will join us soon. They are following behind with wheelbarrows full of food."

She has never defied authority before and the colour rises in her face. But she takes a deep breath and continues speaking. "We had to ride ahead of them to warn you that the Invaders are coming in this direction and may attack us again."

Cries of dismay rise from the crowd that has gathered to greet them.

"We must finish building the palisade right away," Terra adds, looking at her friend with new respect. "They could be here in a couple of days."

"Where did you encounter the enemy?" asks the bearded Elder.

"We didn't. But we received reliable information that they are coming," Laurel replies, blushing even harder.

"From whom?" asks a different Elder, who looks up at them like a turtle from beneath his rounded shoulders.

"From my guardian hawks," Terra announces bravely.

And before anyone can react to this astonishing statement, Aya and Shay swoop overhead, screeching, to land on the roof of the tallest structure in town: the barn the villagers slept in their first night.

The Elders regard the birds with amazement, not knowing what to think. They have read about people communicating with animals in the chronicles of ancient days as well as in prophecies of future times. But they never expected to witness such a thing themselves.

"Terra, my sweet girl, this is not the time for fantasy," her mother reproaches her, appearing from behind a group of villagers.

"I am telling the truth, Mother."

"Why should we believe you, Girl?" asks the Elder who had first spoken.

"Ask her to tell the hawks to do something and they will. They're on our side," Laurel says.

"If they are on our side, show us how they will help us to defeat those masked devils," asks the turtle-man sourly.

Terra looks a little worried until she remembers that Aya had indeed offered to call up an army to assist them.

Can you do it, Aya? she asks. *Can you really raise an army?*

Of course. When the moon rises, we will return.

"In about an hour, when the moon rises, you will see what the birds can do to help us," Terra announces, hoping the trembling in her voice does not reveal her trepidation.

"One *year* would not be enough for you to perform such sorcery!" mutters the turtle-man.

"Do you know what you are doing, Daughter?" Terra's mother asks, her face worried, though she can't help hugging the child who has come home safe to her.

"I hope so, Mother. Meanwhile, I would like to bathe and change my clothes. And look, I found my sketchbook!"

About an hour later the boys arrive, their hands covered with blisters from pushing the wheelbarrows ahead of them. And just as they enter the village, a flock of singing sparrows flies overhead, startling the crowd who stand there waiting.

"All you can offer us is sparrows against arrows," snorts the turtle-man contemptuously.

Next comes a large group of starlings making a tremendous racket, then a dark cloud of crows cawing so loudly the villagers have to cover their ears and finally, majestically, about twenty noble hawks, soaring side by side in silence.

"The girl Terra can speak to birds," says a female Elder, leaning on a cane carved into the shape of a flowering vine. "And that is a sacred and mysterious thing."

"It is enough for me," nods the bearded man.

"Even if she can speak to birds, that doesn't prove that the birds themselves speak the truth!" objects the turtle-man.

"Why would they lie?" asks the first woman Elder.

"And even if they speak the truth, there is no way that pretty feathered creatures can help us defeat men with weapons," the turtle-man continues, determined to reject the extraordinary events that have occurred.

"Of course there is!" says Adam, who has watched the birds soaring overhead with a look of exultation on his face. He goes over to Terra and whispers in her ear. She gives him a hug, and a few minutes later the sparrows fly back, dropping a rain of tiny pebbles onto the roof of the barn. Then the starlings return with larger stones that bounce like hail, and the crows with even larger stones that result in dents and broken boards. Finally, the hawks fly back with rocks suspended from their deadly curving beaks.

"Please don't drop those rocks, O brave and mighty hawks, we beg of you," shouts the bearded Elder. "We have just finished repairing that roof!"

And the hawks veer away.

"We are saved," exclaims the woman with the cane. And then she bursts into tears.

March 18th

Something is wrong with Libby. I mean worse than what's *usually* wrong with her. She's not having epileptic fits anymore, which ought to be a good thing. But she doesn't react when you come into her room, not even when Baxter jumps on the bed to snuggle with her. She never bothers to raise her head to look at anybody or anything. She just sleeps all the time.

The tubes running in and out of her body keep her organs working, so she's still alive, but I keep checking anyway because you can hardly see her chest moving when she breathes. My sister is disappearing, and my parents are freaking out. Despite all their efforts, Libby got a wicked bed sore, technically a "stage III decubitus ulcer of the tuberosity of the ischium," which means there's a red seeping wound on her butt. A visiting nurse had to come and scrape off the infected skin; she gave Libby a shot of anesthetic first and Libby never even woke up, but the tears keep rolling down my mother's face because she believes that she should have been able to prevent this.

Grandma Ruth comes over every day to help my mother and Uncle Martin and my father are consulting every specialist they can find by phone or email, trying to get someone new to see her. We used to rely on our local doctors and the support group for parents of kids with CP, but nobody here seems to know what's going on with her. They claim that she's an "atypical case."

She's so "atypical" that the big guys at the fancy clinics don't know anything either. They love to talk about how much progress they are making and how a cure for CP is on the horizon, etcetera, etcetera, but ask for actual help for an actual patient and they are a lot less confident. They live in a world of statistics and experiments, but my sister isn't a statistic or an experiment. She's a *person*.

I can't concentrate on this journal right now, Mr. Davis. I'm just not into it.

March 22nd

Since I was a little girl I've been drawing pictures for Libby. The wall opposite her bed is covered with corkboard, so it's easy to stick objects up and keep rearranging them into new patterns. We usually display funny family photos, menus from restaurants we've visited, theatre programs, and mementos of special occasions. Dad likes to bring her birds made from weird materials — feathers, straw, tin, felt — that he picks up in craft shops and antique stores. Mum specializes in single earrings (she claims that her body's electromagnetic field repels metal, which is why she loses so much jewellery) and dried flowers. Uncle Martin and Auntie Sam got into the habit of bringing her keychains from every place they visit, and that collection marches down one side of the corkboard in a shiny metal parade. Mum's earrings are strewn about in a much more random pattern. I have to admit I enjoy playing with them. Mum said I could get my ears pierced when I turn thirteen and I'd like to wear some of those mismatched earrings myself. I'm sure Libby won't mind.

Grandma Ruth has never stuck anything on there that I can remember. I'm not sure why. She likes to knit stuff for Libby instead. She makes beautiful blankets, and sweaters, and socks, all in the softest pastel wool that are kind of like extra hugs for my sister when our grandmother isn't here in person. She knits for me too, but not nearly as often as she does for Libby. Maybe because I haven't expressed enough enthusiasm for her efforts, being famously sullen and ungrateful, or maybe because she is able to do other things for me like drive me to swimming lessons or take me shopping for back-to-school clothes.

Anyhow, my own artistic productions in honour of my sister started out as a series of variations on circles and lines, as follows:

(Happy person = one big circle, two small ones, five straight lines, one curved one)

(Happy sun = one big circle, three curved lines, arbitrary number of straight lines)

Why does everyone feel they have to be so upbeat around people like Libby? People like Libby have terrible problems: long term, permanent, never-going-to-get-better problems. We should run around SCREAMING and SMASHING THINGS, not drawing happy pictures. At least then we'd be showing some sympathy for their situation; at least then we'd be acting *real*.

But maybe all the fake cheerfulness we put on — like those nurses in the hospital who ask "And how are we feeling to-day?" — is not for their benefit but for ours. Maybe we are just cheering *ourselves* up because we feel guilty that we don't suffer the way they do. After all, we moan about everything, no matter how trivial — not getting a good grade or a raise at work or a part in a play or whatever — while they are sup-posed to be brave and never complain. Because hey, they're still alive, right?

Another way we are unfair to those who are disabled.

Of course, I'm as bad as everyone else, because for ages I kept on drawing Libby happy cats and happy birds and happy dogs and happy horses.

(Happy flower = three circles, four loopy petals, two loopy leaves, five curved lines)

(Yet another joyful creature)

But eventually I started paying attention to what she wanted to look at, and like any sensible person, she preferred images that were less sentimental. She especially enjoyed pictures that told stories. So I started making a series of cartoons of me and Victoria Lee getting into trouble at school (which is kind of a joke since, if we are famous at all, it's for never doing anything wrong).

When we were younger they included episodes like Vicky being stuck at the top of the jungle gym and afraid to climb down, and me rescuing her wearing a fireman's uniform (this actually happened, although without the uniform). The first cartoon I drew this year was of us getting lost in our new school and our skeletons, covered with spider-webs, being found, years later, by a janitor opening a forgotten broom closet (this is only a slight exaggeration, since the school is enormous and creepy with about twenty different staircases all leading to weird places like autobody shops and pottery studios you didn't even know existed. New students are regularly late because they can't figure out where their classrooms are).

Libby used to love all my artwork, not just the cartoons. But it seems kind of pointless to keep making pictures for her when she won't open her eyes anymore.

March 28th

Something amazing happened today. Libby opened her eyes and looked at me! Dad and I had gone for a walk in the woods with Baxter because it was so beautiful out. The snow had almost all melted. Purple and yellow crocuses were poking their heads up on the south side of our garden and flights of geese were honking overhead on their way north. Dad heard the geese and insisted we go birdwatching in case we could spot some warblers. We didn't see any but it was still nice to get out of the house, although Baxter got filthy and had to be hosed down in the backyard.

Birdwatching with my father reminded me how much Libby used to love those expeditions. So as soon as we got home, I made her a drawing of a hawk in flight.

The piece turned out well, if I do say so myself. It took more than an hour when I was supposed to be doing homework and I worried that it was a poor use of my time, but making art is pretty much the only thing I can do for my sister anymore. She is so fragile I'm afraid to touch her, much less hug her, and nothing I say seems to hold her attention.

Libby's interest used to give meaning to my life. I experienced things with extra intensity so that I could share them with her. For example, I've been going to the Bar and Bat Mitzvahs of the other kids in my class this year. Some of them have made good speeches: Sharon Jacobs related her grandparents' experience of being turned away from two different countries after the war before coming to Canada to the plight of refugees today. That was exactly the kind of thing that Libby liked hearing about. She also used to enjoy gossip about who had the most embarrassing parents or the handsomest big brother or the tackiest dress. But now that she doesn't care what I'm up to, it's hard for me to pay attention to all the details.

Still, despite being pretty sure that my sister couldn't care less what I said or did anymore, I brought my hawk drawing over to her bed tonight and gave her a kiss on her pale cheek.

"Daddy and I went birdwatching today, Libby, and we saw a big red-tailed hawk. It hung around for at least ten minutes, showing off. You would have loved it! But since you weren't with us, I drew a picture for you instead," I said. "Look. Here it is."

For once she opened her eyes. She even tried to say, "Ba."

"Should I hang it up on your corkboard?" I asked.

And then she opened her eyes wide, so I stuck my drawing of the hawk right in the centre of the board where she could easily see it. Except then she went back to sleep.

Still, I thought she had a smile on her face as she dozed off.

April 10th

Flipping through this journal I discovered that both the first entry and the last one were about Libby, and that I told you how one of my earliest memories was her nearly dying when I was four years old.

I guess I was lucky to have her for nine whole years after that, though it doesn't feel lucky right now.

Because my sister died. I thought the last thing she tried to say to me was "Bird," when she looked at the drawing of a hawk I gave her, but maybe what she was saying was "Bye."

As in "Goodbye."

That's why you haven't seen me in class for a couple of weeks, Mr. Davis, although I suspect you already knew that. It's also why I haven't written in this journal for so long. What could I possibly write about? What other "aspects of daily life" could have any "relevance" right now?

English is supposed to be the richest language of them all, with the biggest vocabulary, but sometimes when you are looking for the right word it doesn't exist. We have names for people whose spouses die: a woman's a "widow" and a man's a "widower." Someone who loses both their parents is called an "orphan." But what are you when you lose your sister? How come there's no word for *that*?

It's as though what I feel doesn't count, or my loss is less important than other people's.

Maybe I'm over-reacting, but these days I am mad at everybody: My parents (who are making me go back to school tomorrow); the doctors (who gave up trying to save Libby and just tried to make her "comfortable" instead); my grandmother (who keeps trying to say wise things and then breaking down and sobbing because she's lost so many people in her life that she doesn't believe a word she's saying); Uncle Martin (because he's looking for somebody to blame, as though that will make any difference to how we feel); Vicky (because she never had a sister to lose); the rabbi (because she keeps saying that going ahead with the Bat Mitzvah will help me and my family heal); but most of all God, who is supposed to make everything happen for a higher purpose. The God who made my sister suffer for her whole life and then die without ever being able to walk, or sing, or pat her dog by moving her own hand instead of having us move it for her.

The God who is making me go through the rest of my life without her.

April 12th

We just came back from Libby's funeral. All I remember is a room full of people crying around a wooden casket on a brass stand and then a cemetery full of people crying around a wooden casket in a hole in the ground. Even people I didn't know and people I didn't think cared about my sister were sobbing, like Horrible Hairless Harold, who gave me an actual two-armed hug at the graveside with tears streaming down his face. Then he shook Malcolm's hand and told him how moved he was by his performance.

Malcolm played the guitar and sang "Feeling Good" at the service before we went to the cemetery. He is one of the only people who understands how I'm feeling right now, so I wanted him to participate and my parents said okay. They wanted me to say something also but I'm already talking about Libby at my Bat Mitzvah, which they won't let me cancel even though it's only six weeks away, and I didn't want to do it twice in front of the same people.

Also, I knew that there was no way I could speak today without falling apart.

Besides, Libby wouldn't want to be remembered by speeches; she would have preferred to have people listening to beautiful music and using their imaginations. Libby might not have been able to walk or talk but she had a *great* imagination. After all, she had seventeen years to develop it; seventeen years during which nobody told her to stop making stuff up and be reasonable or forced her to memorize boring facts. Seventeen years during which she was mostly alone with her own thoughts on a journey the rest of us couldn't share with her.

April 20th

I thought I had finished writing in this journal but the most amazing thing just happened. My mother was going through Libby's computer to find that secret project my sister was always working on even though I told her she *shouldn't*, that it was prying, and if Libby had wanted us to see it she would have shared it with us. But it turned out I was wrong (believe it or not, that sometimes happens).

My sister was actually writing a book for me as a thirteenth-birthday present! And my mother knew about it all along, although Libby had never let her read it.

So Mum printed it out and gave it to me.

Best birthday present ever!

It's called *The Discovery of Flight* and it's a fantasy novel set in some unnamed medieval place and time about a hawk and a girl who are linked by telepathy. It's pretty clear that Libby saw herself as the hawk and me as the girl.

Unfortunately, she didn't get to finish the story, but I'm going to. Finishing Libby's book will help me get through the days without her.

I'm not as good a writer as my sister was, not by a long shot, but I'm going to try my best to write something she would have been proud of.

So this is my last journal entry, Mr. Davis. I have a more important project now.

THE DISCOVERY OF FLIGHT
by Elizabeth Adler

THE FINAL CHAPTER, WRITTEN BY SOPHIE ADLER, IN MEMORY OF HER SISTER LIBBY

The Elders draw up a detailed plan of defence and Terra passes it on to the hawks. Construction of the palisade continues at a frantic pace, not even letting up when it gets dark. Workers replace each other in shifts, hammering away by moonlight or by torchlight, building towers at all four corners of the fence that now surrounds the village. They also build solid platforms high up in the pine trees beyond the palisade where hidden archers will be able to wait for their foes.

The hawks agree to sound the alarm when the Invaders are a day's march away. It is Adam's idea that the birds should wait until the Invaders are fairly close before flying over their heads, dropping stones upon them and making as much noise as they can. This is so that the Invaders will associate winged vengeance with the village and realize that Nature itself has risen against them in protest. Maybe this will also persuade them not to pluck feathers from innocent birds to decorate their horrible masks.

Meanwhile the archers in the trees will start to shoot, aiming for the Invaders' arms and hands, making it impossible for them to lift their own weapons. Unlike their enemies, the villagers are determined to avoid as much bloodshed as possible. They don't want to kill people because violence always leads to more violence and they hope to live in peace.

Sol thinks that the archers should set their arrows on fire to make them even more frightening but the birds are outraged by this suggestion. This would risk igniting a blaze in the forest and destroying the homes of other creatures.

The boy apologizes to the birds, admitting he hadn't thought about the potential consequences.

You humans have a lot to learn, Aya mutters to Terra.

He means well, Terra protests. *He's just young.*

He might be young but Sol is one of the best archers in the village, so as soon as the alarm is sounded he takes up his position in the first line of defence. Terra and Adam are among a group stationed closer to the village.

"I *have* to do this," Terra insists, when her parents beg her not to volunteer. "Aya and her friends are endangering themselves to save our lives. It is only fair that I take the same risks as they do."

"But you are not a skilled archer," her father argues.

"And unlike a bird, you cannot fly away," her mother adds.

"You taught me to throw the dagger well. Hopefully that will be enough."

With heavy hearts, they watch Terra leave, then take up their own positions behind the palisade. Being old and frail they are not expected to engage in combat, but they have stacked wood upon which to boil a great pot of water. Ropes and pulleys around the pot's handles will allow them to heave it up and dump it over the fence onto any attackers who make it that far. Everyone has a role to play in this battle, even the smallest children, who have gathered stones and pebbles to arm the birds who are flying about them, perching on their shoulders and eating from their hands.

The village dogs and cats have learned they are not to attack the birds; lessons taught as much by the swooping hawks as by their human masters.

Shay's prediction proves true: the Invaders arrive three days after Terra and the others return from scavenging. It seems to Terra that they are like a terrible disease that returns to kill a person after a short period of remission. Leading them is the giant who built the funeral pyre in their old village — a monster whose bulging arms are covered with black and red tattoos of skeletons and fire and swords, of lightning bolts and snakes. His face is painted black and red as well, so that his teeth, filed to jagged points, look impossibly white, and he wears a red cloak covered with black and white feathers.

As soon as the giant nears the village a mighty wind is raised by a thousand wing-beats and stones of every size — some as small as blueberries, others as large as plums — fall upon him and his gang. At the same time, a hail of arrows flies at them from every direction. Many Invaders fall, howling and clutching their arms and legs. Some turn pale under their war paint and stand frozen on the spot; others run back the way they came.

Ignoring the havoc behind him, ignoring even the blood oozing from his own shoulder as he pulls an arrow out of it and then snaps it across one enormous knee, the giant turns and scrutinizes the area. Immediately to his left he sees a bough rustle slightly and, without hesitation, flings his spear at the spot. There is a howl of pain and a boy topples out of the tree clutching his chest, the shaft of the spear protruding between his fingers. Exultant, the giant runs on towards the village, pulling a double-headed axe out of his belt, looking for someone else to kill.

Seeing Sol fall to his death from the tree, Terra is unable to suppress a cry of grief. That cry betrays her position to the giant, who turns in her direction. But before he reaches the spot where she clings to a branch, before the axe can leave his fist, Aya swoops down upon him in a fury of wings and talons and teeth, ripping off his left ear and raking the skin from the side of his jaw.

This does not stop him; nothing can. He is a machine made of pure rage. He swings his axe over his head even as the bird tries to peck out his eyes, and connects with one of her beautiful wings, slicing right through the feathers to bone. Aya falls to the ground, stunned and bleeding. But as the giant prepares to cut off her head, still screeching curses at him, a dagger flies into him, piercing his heart.

The axe falls from his hand and he topples over like a tree.

Terra climbs down from her perch, shouting Aya's name over and over as she hurries to the wounded bird. Nobody tries to stop her. The rest of the Invaders ran away when their captain fell and the woods are filled with an eerie silence; a silence louder than the noise of battle.

You saved my life, Aya, the girl whispers to the hawk, whose golden eyes are already beginning to glaze over.

I'm glad. Now I can die in peace.

Please don't leave me.

What use is a hawk who can't fly?

But you are my sister. *How can I live without you?*

My time has come. Goodbye, Terra.

Goodbye, Terra replies to the hawk whose broken body lies in her lap.

And with one hand, she gently closes those golden eyes forever.

THE END

ACKNOWLEDGEMENTS

When I was in university, I volunteered at a residential home for severely disabled children and adolescents. A teenage girl there who was completely locked in, unable to move or speak, had the most beautiful and intelligent eyes I'd ever seen. This story is inspired by her and is for her, though I no longer remember her name.

Thanks for financial support and emotional encouragement during the writing of this book to the Toronto Arts Council and the Ontario Arts Council, and to Cormorant Books, Second Story Press, and Wolsak & Wynn publishers. Special gratitude to Luciana Ricciutelli, my wonderful editor at Inanna, and to everyone else at the press, especially Val Fullard for the stunning cover.

For other kinds of support, grateful thanks to my friends and family, especially those who read and commented on early versions of the manuscript: Helena Aalto, Rachel Klein, Zoe Migicovsky, Robert Priest, Michelle Soicher, Meira and Yamit Shem Tov, Amy Tomkins, and Yasemin Uçar.

Photo: Toan Klein

Susan Glickman is the author of six volumes of poetry, most recently *The Smooth Yarrow* (2012), three novels for adults, most recently *Safe as Houses* (2015), the "*Lunch Bunch*" trilogy of children's books, and *The Picturesque & the Sublime: A Poetics of the Canadian Landscape* (1998). She works as a freelance editor, primarily of academic books, and teaches creative writing in the continuing education program at Ryerson University.